"Any clues to my identity?" she asked wistfully

"I did find these two brown paper bags on the plane." He emptied the contents onto the comforter revealing an odd assortment of jewelry, including a pocket watch and a plain gold band.

"What's wrong?" she asked before spotting the ring. Suddenly Garrett caught her hand and looked closely at her fingers. Her hand felt lost in his grasp; his touch was almost a caress. At first she wondered if he was making a pass, but after a few seconds he let go.

Janiver noticed the band and examined it. "Could this mean I'm married?"

"Possibly." He seemed as disturbed by her predicament as she was.

MARIEL KIRK started reading breakfast cereal boxes at the age of four and continues to absorb all written matter that passes before her eyes. As a university student, she went to Ankara, Turkey, to help establish a new university there. The experience opened her eyes to world politics and provided her with background material for her romance novels and children's stories. The author is married, has four children and lives in Colorado.

Prisoner of
Shadow Mountain

Mariel Kirk

Harlequin Books

TORONTO • NEW YORK • LONDON
AMSTERDAM • PARIS • SYDNEY • HAMBURG
STOCKHOLM • ATHENS • TOKYO • MILAN

ISBN 0-373-02786-9

Harlequin Romance first edition September 1986

CHAPTER ONE

THE SKY, CLEAR AND BLUE, looked peaceful enough when Janiver Parmalee taxied her red plane down the grass landing strip to lift gracefully above telephone wires and electric power lines. Banking to the left brought the nose around, and in moments she was flying west, toward the mountains. She waved in the general direction of the small hangar and the stubby figure in blue coveralls. The pristine air permitted her a magnificent view of the front range of the Colorado Rockies. Snowcapped peaks rose before her, contrasting with the bland farmland nestled east of the foothills. November's brisk winds had erased Denver's smog.

Below her were two worlds in conflict. Denver's Old West image had given way to high-rise office buildings housing oil companies. Influences from both coasts shaped the queen city of the plains, with often confusing results.

Janiver kept one foot in each world.

She still belonged to her father's world and Floyd's, and she understood their repeated lament.

"They're messing up Colorado," Floyd would announce, folding the morning paper and reaching for another cup of coffee.

And her father would nod in sober agreement. "Speculators sacrificing Colorado for dollars." Then they would shake their heads over the sins of the nebulous "they."

"It's all right, Floyd," Janiver would soothe the balding little man, his face creased and wind worn. "Colorado is still a great place to live." She knew Floyd believed it, too.

Janiver was equally at home in the other world, the fast-paced modern world of international business and cosmopolitan elegance. Just the day before, she'd been sent out from Denver to Jackson Hole, Wyoming, on a fashion show. She and several other models had shown hand-knit Scandinavian wear for a gathering of executive wives. Janiver shook her head, remembering the deluge of orders; those women knew how to spend money—and they had superb taste. Floyd hadn't raised any objections about taking the plane to the Wyoming assignment, but for some reason, he'd been against this flight.

"I tell you, Janiver, I feel it in my bones. You shouldn't go. At least wait until morning."

"Quit fussing, Floyd! See, the sky is clear! Allen says Steamboat is fine, and the skiing is fantastic! Powder three feet deep. I can't resist a free weekend at a luxury condo," she'd said with an impish grin, knowing he distrusted the sport of skiing altogether. Despite Floyd's misgivings, Janiver was now airborne, and her ski equipment was stowed next to her suitcase.

"It's that boyfriend of yours, Janiver," he had grumbled.

"I know your friends are your own business, Jan, but there's something about him . . ."

"As I recall, you didn't approve of the last one, either, Floyd. You're just not tuned in to my taste in men!"

Besides, she had never called Allen Tobin her "boyfriend"—whatever that term meant. She had been dating Allen off and on for the past several months, but nothing serious had developed between them. They were friends—from her point of view, anyway.

As a well-paid model, appearing to be supremely self-assured had disadvantages. Men either came on so strong that she was compelled to keep them at arm's length, or they assumed her social calendar was full and never bothered to ask her out at all.

So for the time being, it was comfortable and convenient to have Allen as a reliable escort, as someone to go around with. Perhaps—later—their relationship would develop beyond the "just friends" stage. Allen was becoming more and more insistent, pushing her for further intimacy, but Janiver still held back. She simply wasn't sure about her feelings.

There wasn't a cloud along the front range. The only marring of the translucent blue was a faint smudge beyond Mount

Evans. The feeling Floyd had in his bones must have been wrong, she thought. This was a gorgeous day.

"Floyd, you sweet old worrywart," she murmured now. "You just didn't want me to see Allen." She glanced down at the two paper bags he'd placed on the seat beside her, along with a folded newspaper.

Janiver's red turtleneck sweater and pink down jacket emphasized her classic blondness. A red baseball cap was perched atop long silky hair, tied back in a practical ponytail. At the fashion show the day before she had been groomed and polished to glossy perfection; now she wore a minimum of makeup and her oldest blue jeans.

She had been flying for about half an hour, when she realized that the texture of the air outside had thickened slightly. She looked warily around but saw no danger; it was just that she couldn't see the valleys below quite as clearly now.

With luck she could ski several runs before nightfall, as some of the slopes were lighted. This was going to be fun!

Janiver was planning which après-ski outfit to wear that evening and how to fix her hair, when snow began to fall. First tiny, innocent flakes blurred visibility slightly, then suddenly snow was everywhere.

Visibility degenerated to zero. There was only white all around the plane. The smudge she'd seen behind Mount Evans had turned into a storm. Mentally she offered Floyd an apology—she'd never distrust his bones again. Then she gave her full attention to the crisis at hand. She checked the navigation chart, scanned the instrument panel. Technically everything was as it should be, but the ground had disappeared.

She dared not fly blind; there was too great a risk that she would smash right into the ground or the side of a mountain. As the small craft hit an air pocket it bounced like a hiccup, and Janiver grabbed at the controls to compensate for the sudden jolt.

Her headphones crackled and she switched on the transmitter, asking for a weather report. Inanely the answer came, "Snow in North Park."

"Thanks, mate," she muttered, "considering I'm surrounded by the beautiful stuff." A slight pressure from her hand sent the plane higher as she attempted to get above the squall. But altitude did not bring her to open sky. The snow curtain still imprisoned her.

She could scarcely see to the wing's tip. The dials gave small comfort as she once more fought disorientation. The altimeter indicated she was still safely above fourteen thousand feet, and she pointed the plane's nose upward again.

But now the aircraft seemed sluggish and heavy; it didn't feel right. Squinting, she looked out the window. Through intermittent holes in the snow curtain, she saw the jagged white fingers that clung to the wings. Ice!

Ice had formed along the wings, adding weight, slowing her climb. Ice, the silent extra passenger all pilots dreaded. She should have been more careful, should have heeded Floyd's warnings.

Suddenly she felt fear—unfamiliar, unwanted, real. Her heart was in her throat, her hands sweaty inside the leather gloves. The cockpit was suddenly chilled and her feet were cold. *This is nonsense,* she scolded herself. *Straighten up! Fear kills pilots, you numskull!*

She monitored the instrument panel again, peering out in a vain effort to pierce the snow curtain. The sluggishness of the plane forced her to admit that she was in danger. She was flying blind through the highest mountain range in North America, with deadly ice pulling her plane down.

Janiver's emotions rose and dipped in rhythm with the fluctuations of her thoughts.

I'll be out of this soon, she comforted herself. *In just a few minutes there will be blue skies and sunshine. Colorado weather is like that.*

Her mind reached desperately for bits of lore, anything Floyd might have said, anything she might have gleaned from pilot talk around the hangar, anything that might help.

The first rule, of course, was not to panic. It wouldn't be easy. There was no point in denying that the plane was resisting her efforts to get back on course.

She dared not go lower, because unseen peaks waited beneath her. Or were those peaks actually level with her at this very moment?

"A Fox One Zero to ground." She spoke firmly into the radio receiver, waiting for a response. None came.

Now she detected a difference in the cabin's slant, as though some giant were pushing gently on the plane's nose.

She would go down unless the squall ended—and ended quickly.

The engine's pulse skipped a beat. If the wings went she didn't have a chance.

Her mind went blank—empty as the receiver.

"Mayday! Mayday!" Though she spoke to a deaf world, she followed the cardinal rule of emergency procedure—send distress signals as long as possible.

The white blindness still clung to her windshield.

A treacherous and deadly calm settled over her. No use fighting, she admitted. She'd have to put down as best she could, make a crash landing.

For weeks snowfall had been heavier than usual in the Rockies. Daily ski reports documented the unusual depth of the snow base awaiting gleeful skiers. *A nice soft landing for me and* Little Susy, Janiver throught wryly. But there was doubt in her narrowed eyes and the set of her mouth.

A parade of unrelated thoughts marched through her head. Last winter a plane had gone down on a snowpacked mountainside and the passengers had survived. They had been rescued a week later, having kept fairly warm inside the insulated cockpit. She was suddenly aware of her hands and feet, already too cold for comfort.

She remembered Allen's phone call. *"Don't be late, Jan. I can't wait to see you."* Well, he'd have to wait—perhaps a very long time.

All around the plane danced the tiny specks of white death. The altimeter indicated she was now below fourteen thousand feet. Only luck, blind luck, kept her from colliding with a mountain. Falling snow was indistinguishable from snow-clad slopes.

Surprisingly her thoughts now were clear and sharp. She was conscious of the danger all around her—in the storm, in the altitude, in the plane's fragility. *Life is so tenuous,* she thought with philosophical detachment.

The seconds seemed to pass in slow motion. There seemed to be time for all sorts of thoughts, about the world, about her life, about the plane, about the recent fashion show in Wyoming, about Allen....

Janiver did not confront the possibility that she might be hurtling toward her death. Her mind was fixed on the sensations of the past few seconds. *Yes,* she noted dispassionately, *it's true. In a crisis time does slow down. When I get out of here I'll think more about that.*

Then a shadow loomed, filling the windshield with a solid whiteness. She no longer sought to avoid the inevitable. The right wing sheared off; the plane tilted. And a whiter, deeper mass awaited her.

The plane's nose dug into the snow. Janiver could hear metal ripping against rocks, feel the thud of impact. Her body was pushed upward, then sideways. Her head bumped something hard. She cried out, but there was no one to hear.

Then came blackness, and silence . . . and cold.

Snow continued to fall, covering the red plane with exquisitely shimmering flakes, knitting them into a soft shroud that shut out the world.

She felt cold silence all around her. She tried to form speech, but there were no sounds in the velvet darkness behind her closed eyelids. She lay on a cold dark planet, her body aching, one side of her head the center of a sharp pain. Then she drifted away. Drifted. Floated. Shivered.

WARMTH BEGAN TO CREEP back into her almost lifeless body, slowly, hesitantly.

Her eyelids were like stones. At last she succeeded in forcing her eyes open, focusing with difficulty on a lamp beside the bed where she lay. A deliciously warm bed.

Memories flitted past—of intense cold, of movement, of strange sounds, of a voice—a man's voice. She didn't know why, but the voice seemed to have some connection with the new warmth she was feeling. The dream must have been a very long one.

Painfully she shifted her gaze to the end of the bed and beyond, trying to take in her surroundings, registering images on her numbed brain.

The room was a large one, with a high ceiling braced by peeled logs aged to a mellow golden hue. She found that she was covered with a blue down-filled comforter and that she lay on a bed placed against one of the longer walls. A small, steady fire burned in the massive stone fireplace at the opposite end of the room. Adjoining the fireplace were shelves of books and stereo equipment. The room's overall effect was of honest comfort.

Where was she?

Pain returned as she moved her head. A few feet to the side of the bed a door stood ajar. She guessed it led to a bathroom. Diagonally across the big room was a heavier door that presumably led outside. She heard a groan and realized, surprised, that it must have come from her.

Her head throbbed. The dull ache radiated through her body at the slightest move, so she lay very still.

"Where is this?" She experimented weakly, haltingly, with the words; her mouth seemed unaccustomed to speech.

No one answered.

The room appeared to be L-shaped, with the small branch of the L hidden from her sight. Perhaps there was someone around that corner.

The pain in her head and upper body constrained her movements, and she felt an unfamiliar sense of being a prisoner inside her own body.

She sniffed, tempted by an appetizing aroma.

Food!

"Hey! Hello! Anyone!" Her voice dissipated a few feet away, dying in the silence.

Whatever was cooking smelled utterly delicious. Her struggle to raise her head from the pillow was briefly successful, before the pain pushed her down again. Her eyes closed, and she rested from the effort. Even taking a deep breath was excruciating. She drowsed again, floating away into a gray fog.

After a time something penetrated her dazed mind, some far-off noise. Concentrating carefully, she identified the sound of heavy footsteps stamping outside, then opened her eyes to watch in blurred fascination as the heavy wooden door swung open and a man entered, followed by a dog.

She saw that the man was tall and broad shouldered, bundled in a bright hunter-orange down jacket and a heavy knit cap, pulled over his ears. Snow clung to his blue jeans, which were tucked into heavy boots. The dog was a great golden beauty, a mixture of retriever and another large breed.

She watched curiously as the man removed his coat and hat and stowed them in the closet. Fear tinged her curiosity and she struggled to sit up, but a sudden wave of pain ended the attempt. She fell back on the pillow and a moan escaped her swollen lips. The sound and her movement drew the attention of man and dog to where she lay.

"Well! Hello!" His voice was deep and pleasant. A wide smile lighted his bearded face as he strode toward the bed. He was tall, very tall, indeed, filling her entire field of vision. His hair and short beard were a warm brown, his eyes shadowed.

"Hello." She answered him in a hoarse, rasping voice. A drink of water; she needed water. She licked her lips, feeling how misshapen they were.

She hadn't the faintest idea who the man was. She understood that somehow she had been injured, and she waited patiently for memory to rush into her consciousness, but it didn't.

An outdoor chill surrounded him like a cloud, and she snuggled deeper beneath the comforter. Who was he? Did she know him? Was he her husband? Her lover? She stared at him, her eyes huge and smoky with pain.

"You're a lucky girl," he commented, leaning over her.

Close up, his beard appeared to be a recent addition to his face, and she saw that his eyes were a deep blue, quite startling with his brown hair.

"Why?" she croaked. "Lucky" did not seem appropriate for the pain that racked her. She frowned. "Where is this?"

His brows shot up and he dragged a nearby chair toward the bed. He straddled it and leaned his chin on his hands, regarding her with interest. The dog sat on her haunches beside him, head cocked to one side, brown eyes fixed on the newcomer.

"Water?" he asked. Her lips felt dry and cracked.

He reached for a glass on the table. Tentatively she put out her hand, but he came around and held it to her lips, one arm supporting her, his other guiding the glass to her mouth.

The cool water was heavenly, sliding smoothly down her parched throat. She sank back, watching him, trying to clear the fuzz from her mind, wondering who he was. What was his name? What was he to her?

"Thank you." Her throat no longer felt so sore. "Where is this? What happened?"

"You don't remember the accident?" He smiled, but his smile was perfunctory, without any warmth.

She licked her lips. "An automobile accident?" Her voice sounded thin and reedy.

He looked unbelieving. "No, not an automobile accident," he said quietly.

She creased her forehead in bewilderment.

"You were tangled in the wreckage of a small airplane halfway up the saddle back."

She simply stared at him, too tired and pain filled to comprehend. What he said was preposterous. He was lying, of course. But why? If she could only remember what had happened.

"Head hurt?" he asked.

"Yes, terribly." She closed her eyes, shutting him out. Shutting out the questions.

She heard him go into what she assumed was the bathroom, then return. Forcing her eyelids open, she saw him standing at the bedside with a white tablet and more water.

"This will help," he assured her.

She gritted her teeth as pain seared through her when she swallowed. She sank back, exhausted, and he sat down once more, linking his hands as he leaned toward her.

"Now," he said briskly, "what's your name and where were you going? Someone is undoubtedly frantic, wondering what's happened to you."

She kept her eyes closed for a moment. Her eyelids felt so very heavy. She slowly raised them and concentrated her gaze on his face.

"I don't know."

"What's that supposed to mean? You don't know!" His tone was sarcastic and he spoke louder than before.

Inside her mind she formed the words, but when she opened her mouth there was no sound. She was so tired. Her eyes closed and she slept once more.

She felt much better when she opened them again. Fire danced brightly in the fireplace. The golden dog lay quietly on the hearthrug and someone was moving around in the part of the room hidden from her view. She had no way of knowing how long she might have slept.

She was not aware that she had made any sound, but almost immediately the strange man appeared beside her bed. And with him, confusion also returned.

Who was he?

"Hey, there, sleepyhead." There was no hint of irritation in his voice now. As though there had been no break in their conversation, she croaked, "What accident?"

"Who are you?" he countered, his voice hard.

She enunciated slowly and distinctly because she didn't want to repeat her words again. "I have no idea who I am, where I'm from, how I got here, or who you are." The strain of talking left her gasping.

His dark brows rose and he whistled in disbelief. "Mmm? 'Beautiful blonde discovered unconscious in plane wreck. Loses memory when rescued by stranded mountain man.' Great story line for a cheap novel, or banner headline for some supermarket rag sheet." He paused. "You don't expect me to swallow that, do you?" His tone had become harsh and unfriendly, almost hostile.

"Why don't you believe me?" She was mystified.

He stared down at her as though trying to read her mind. She smiled faintly at the idea of someone reading a mind that was as empty as a deserted house.

"Any soap opera is more believable than that," he said coldly.

She heaved herself onto one elbow, then turned slightly to face him.

"What does that mean?" Her cheeks blazed with sudden color; her eyes sparked with anger.

"I suggest you start at the beginning," he advised.

"Beginning of what?" she snapped. "I'm telling you, whoever you are, my mind is blank! Empty! Zero! I remember nothing before I woke up here in your damned stupid bed!"

He frowned, two straight lines plowing his forehead. He began again.

"What's your name?" The tone was patient, as if he were speaking to a child.

She shook her head, then winced at the motion. "You really don't believe me, do you?"

He turned and strode angrily into the hidden part of the room.

"Are you hungry?" he called. Apparently the question and answer session had ended—for now. She had no doubt he would resume the inquisition when it suited him.

"I'm famished," she answered.

"We eat out here." The voice was totally unsympathetic.

She fumed to herself, but with immense effort pushed back the comforter. She was mildly surprised to find herself clad in a pair of men's blue flannel pajamas. Her thoughts began to spin around in dizzy confusion.

The texture of the braided rug on the floor beside the bed was comforting to her bare feet. As she slid off the bed, the pajama leg bunched up, revealing ugly purple bruises on her shin. She looked for a robe of some sort, saw none, then gathered the comforter around her shoulders. Her legs felt like rubber bands. She tottered to the corner of the room, where it angled off into the previously concealed area.

As she had already guessed from the aroma of cooking, this was a combined kitchen and dining room. She saw that it was superbly equipped with gleaming appliances and a variety of up-to-date kitchen accessories. In the center of the space was a round wooden table set for two. Beside the stove the tall man ladled steaming liquid into bowls.

A wave of pain shot through her, and her legs refused to support her any further. She teetered on the brink of a gray-black haze. Before she could slide to the floor he had put the bowl down and with two giant strides was beside her, holding her, preventing her from falling.

"Laurie!" His voice was full of concern, quite unlike his impersonal tone of a few minutes earlier.

The room faded and she floated once again through space. And then she had to do it all again—traverse the dark familiar planet. It wasn't cold this time and her eyelids were not so heavy. When she forced them open, she was aware of strong arms holding her, carrying her to the bed, gently laying her down and covering her.

"I'm sorry," she murmured to the broad chest.

The man cursed. *What's wrong with him now,* she thought crossly.

"I said, I'm sorry," she repeated faintly.

"I'm angry with myself, Laurie, not you." The voice in the fog was gentle.

" 'Laurie'?" she questioned. "Is that my name?"

"Don't worry about that now. I'll bring dinner in here, and we'll talk after you've eaten."

"Is it dinnertime?" she asked, noticing that the windowpane beneath the blind was black. But he had already left. From the sound of things, he was assembling plates and glasses.

Soon he reappeared. "You need food. You've had nothing since I found you two days ago."

Two days?

His words bounced off her mind as she looked longingly at the tray, at the bowl of steaming stew and cup of hot chocolate. The sight and smell of the food crowded out all other thoughts. She would eat first, ask questions later.

"My compliments to the chef," she commented, savoring the rich beefy taste and the hot buttered bread.

"Thank you, ma'm'selle." He had set his own tray on the edge of the bureau and was eating heartily.

When hunger was partially satisfied she laid down her spoon. "So—how did I get here? Wherever this is."

"You got caught in the storm and crashed up on the mountain. But finish your dinner. There'll be plenty of time for explanations," he said nonchalantly, as if a plane crash were a common everyday occurrence.

She had another spoonful of stew. "What's your name?" she asked.

"Garrett Collier." He spread butter on his bread.

The name meant nothing to her.

"What's my name?"

"Remember? I asked you that question and you claimed not to know." He was at least courteous this time around.

Warmth and food had strengthened her, but whatever part of her mind housed the past was empty.

"I don't know!" she repeated turning to him.

"Truthfully?" His inscrutable face made her uneasy.

"Why would I lie?"

"I'd have no way of knowing that." The coldness was back in his voice.

"You're mighty suspicious!" she accused.

At that he grinned. "You're improving if you're worried about my being rude."

As far as she could tell, her life had begun when she'd awakened in this room a few hours earlier, and ended with this moment—now. Before that there was nothing. She had no memory of who she'd been or what had happened before she'd woken up in this bed. Before she'd seen this man who sat so calmly stowing away food.

"Garrett Collier, didn't you come across any luggage or papers when you found me?"

She felt so much stronger now she could almost ignore the sharp pains tormenting every move.

Garrett handed her a glass of white wine.

"I did find two brown paper bags and a newspaper, but the snow wet them through. I haven't looked at them."

"You actually found me in the wreckage of an airplane?"

"Yes, I actually did." He paused; a pensive look came over his face. "You honestly don't know your identity, do you?"

"No, I honestly don't," she imitated him. Her light tone fought off the specter of depression lurking in the back of her mind.

He looked reflective as he went to jab at the logs in the fireplace with a poker. Golden flames rose obediently at his touch. The dog, still sprawled on the hearthrug, stirred in her sleep, though Garrett skirted carefully around her.

"I can go back to look for clues when I get a chance," he said, as though he might not be able to fit the search into his schedule for some time.

"Surely I'll remember."

"It's the stuff of melodrama, isn't it?" He smiled. "Amnesia is seldom found outside bad fiction."

"But what if I don't?" Panic edged her voice.

"There's nothing to be done now. The access road is blocked by an avalanche, so we couldn't get off the mountain even if we wanted to." She noticed he'd said "we." Well, at least they were on the same team. "We have food and firewood for three months. We may as well make the best of the situation."

"Three months!" she yelped.

"Where are you planning to go?" He turned to watch her closely.

"Touché," she answered soberly, pausing. "And what are you doing up here?"

"Several things. It's a long story, and boring, really. You're damned lucky I'm here, or you'd still be out there in that twisted pile of junk. You'd probably have been dead by now."

The fact that she might have died seemed to haunt him, and his intensity puzzled her. She, too, was glad she was alive. Though she was bruised, she seemed little the worse. And in the safe, cozy warmth of this room, she could easily believe that her memory would soon return. The dimly remembered sensation of cold darkness suddenly made her shiver.

"I don't mean to pry, and I do thank you for saving my life," she apologized.

"Gratitude isn't necessary." He finished his wine, poured himself a refill. "Let's stop sparring. I'm not even sure what we're arguing about."

Nor was she. She reached out to meet the hand he offered. As her hand disappeared into his, she felt a moment of panic. She somehow knew that she must not let herself be swallowed up by anyone.

"If I heard the story all over again, would it jog my memory, do you think? Tell me how you found me. Did I say anything?" She lay back on the pillow.

He ignored her question. "You need rest."

"I need answers. I was going somewhere, and now—here I am in a vacuum."

He paced, roaming between the fireplace and the bed. "Questions, questions. That's a good sign, I suppose," he said with a grin. A few more turns along the carpet and finally he stood beside the bed again. He eyed her speculatively, as if wondering whether he should say what was on his mind. Then he took a deep breath.

"I thought you were dead," he said.

His tone was flat, but she sensed that the outward calm hid some strong emotion.

"Start at the beginning," she requested gently. He sat down and cleared his throat.

In the late afternoon, he told her, he had heard an airplane flying low. *"Poor fool, I hope he makes it,"* he'd thought, then hearing nothing further, had dismissed the episode.

The heavy snowfall had caused him problems, too. His truck had got stuck in a deep drift when he had been hauling firewood, and it had taken him hours to finally dig himself out.

"That evening," he said, "I kept thinking about the plane I'd heard. The next morning was sunny, so I had a quick breakfast and set out on my cross-country skis with Winnie— that's my dog's name—to have a look around. Just in case."

He described how he'd taken his time, enjoying the delights of skiing through the majestic white silence. To be truthful, he hadn't expected to find anything except pines, new snow, a few elk and deer and lots of quiet—the wonderful crackling silence of the high country in winter.

"If I did find something, I didn't expect to be able to do much," he said, "except notify the authorities. Planes colliding with mountains don't ordinarily leave many options." At that his lips twisted in a mirthless smile. He paused, went to the fridge and came back with an opened beer.

"I never would have seen the plane if it hadn't been for Winnie."

Janiver began to interrupt, but was silenced by the agony on his face. He was absorbed in reliving the emotion of the moment he'd discovered the wreckage.

"Winnie ran ahead, falling into the powder, walking on the drifts, having a great time. Suddenly she barked and raced up toward a stand of trees. Then she started digging frantically in a snowbank. When I caught up, she'd uncovered a patch of red metal."

"The plane?"

He nodded, his eyes fixed somewhere beyond her.

She struggled to remember, to fit his story into the blankness of her memory, but there was nothing.

He tipped back his head to drink deeply from the beer. "The dog had found the tail section of a small plane. It was hard to tell how long it had been there, but I couldn't rule out that it was the one I'd heard the day before." He drained his beer and stood holding the empty can, his eyes on nothing.

She shivered involuntarily.

"Cold?" He was instantly solicitous.

She shook her head, winced. "No."

After a while he went on. "Probably ten minutes later, I found the door. The snow was three or four feet deep, mostly powder, and it kept sliding into where I'd already dug. And my equipment was rather primitive—two hands and one ski."

She could visualize the scene.

"Winnie kept giving out little barks as though she'd found something exciting. I yelled, hoping for an answer, but there were only echoes from the mountains." Seconds of silence ticked by, and she could see the emotion on his face—see how much he must have dreaded finding someone he thought was dead inside the plane.

At last Garrett resumed his story. "I finally got the door open, and looked inside. There you were, thrown against the far wall like a rag doll. Your hair was spread out against the window and there was blood in it. There was dried blood on the side of your face, too."

Again he paused a long moment, without looking at her.

CHAPTER TWO

"I THOUGHT YOU WERE DEAD," he said, his voice toneless, a faraway look still in his eyes. Then he told her how he'd seen the nearly imperceptible rise of her chest and a tiny cloud of breath in the cold still air.

"I remember shouting out an incredulous prayer of thanks. 'God in heaven, the girl is alive,' I cried! But barely. Your skin was icy to the touch."

He told her how he'd worked frantically to extricate her, hoping it wouldn't be dangerous to move her, knowing he had no choice.

"I crawled inside the plane to retrieve you," he said. "Then I straightened your body, and soon had you lying outside in the bright sunshine. I hadn't been sure what to do next, but in desperation I grabbed at the plane's warped door and from somewhere got the strength to wrest it from its hinges."

From that he'd fashioned a crude sled, he explained. He hadn't searched the craft thoroughly, so if there were any clues to her identity he could have missed them. But he'd been in a hurry to get her to his cabin.

"I had no idea you'd wake up with a blank space between your ears!" he teased.

"No clues at all about my identity?" she asked wistfully.

"None." He frowned. "Except..." He stopped and disappeared for a minute around the corner of the room, returning with two brown paper bags, tops folded and stapled.

"Shall I open them?" he asked.

"Go ahead," she agreed. He pulled open the larger one and looked inside.

"This will solve everything," he announced with a broad smile, bringing out a tattered ham sandwich on whole wheat bread, holding it up with a comical expression on his face.

She laughed. "Is there a sales slip?"

"Nothing," he reported.

"What's in the other one?" she asked impatiently.

He tore it open and emptied the contents onto the comforter, revealing an odd assortment of jewelry, including a man's pocket watch and a plain gold ring.

She reached for them—the small shining links to her past life. But he caught her hand, looking closely at her fingertips.

"What's wrong?" she asked anxiously, twisting to see what he might be finding of interest. His hand was large and strong, and hers felt lost in his grasp.

He inspected her short polished nails, his touch almost a caress. At first she wondered if he was making a pass, but after a few seconds, he threw her a curious look and laid her hand back on the bed. She was glad he had relinquished it voluntarily. She couldn't have resisted him—not in her condition.

She examined the gold ring for initials or other hints of its origin.

"Could this mean I'm married?" she asked.

"Possibly."

"This is no help at all." Her voice was low, and tight as a bowstring, and she pushed the baubles away.

She was more confused than ever. The wall in her mind separating her from her past was without crack or crevice.

At least, she thought, *I know how I got here.* That is, if Garrett Collier's story was true. He had no reason to lie, had he? He seemed as puzzled by her predicament as she was.

The other jewelry in the brown bag was unimportant when compared with the gold band, which looked like a wedding ring.

There was also a delicate gold chain, and earrings with diamond chips that winked like ice crystals.

"The jewelry looks like fairly good quality," she commented.

"Why so casually thrown into a paper sack?" he asked.

"I can't imagine." They looked at each other helplessly.

The comforter had fallen away from her shoulders, allowing the lamplight to play over her bruised face and her slim pale neck. Her honey-colored hair tumbled around her face and shoulders, almost hiding the wound on the side of her face.

Looking at her, Garrett caught his breath.

"I guess you can call me 'hey, you,'" she said lightly, hiding the tightly wound tension she felt inside.

"I call you 'Laurie,'" he said.

She looked at him sharply. One minute he seemed distant and the next—she wasn't sure. "Really? Why?"

"I don't know, but for some reason that name came into my head. I have to call you something, and it sounds better somehow than 'miss,' or 'hey, you,' don't you think?"

"I suppose." she said with a smile. "Well, Laurie who?"

"Which do you prefer, Smith or Doe?"

"Doesn't make much difference, does it?"

"Not at this point." He watched her closely, waiting. Waiting for what?

"My mind is like a sieve. Tell me your name again."

"Garrett Collier."

"Have I ever heard of you?"

"Meaning what?" he hedged.

"Are you famous?"

At that he threw back his head and laughed. "Good heavens, no."

"This is silly," she exclaimed.

"What is?"

"Not remembering."

"Yes," he agreed amiably. "It is, isn't it?"

"What will I do?" Surely this would pass and she would be a real person again, with an identity of her own.

"First, rest," he advised.

"Sounds sensible. I don't feel up to momentous decisions right now. But small ones, like sleeping, I can probably cope with."

She suddenly realized she was in his bed. "Where will you sleep?"

"The couch has been quite comfortable."

"Do you have enough blankets?"

"No problem."

He gathered their dinner dishes and carried them into the other room. Soon he was accumulating blankets from drawers and spreading them on the couch, banking the fire and turning off the lights.

"Good night, Garrett Collier," she called when he had turned out the lamp by his makeshift bed. She snuggled into her mound of blankets, feeling warm and secure. Everything would be all right—hadn't Garrett said so?

"Good night, Laurie Smith Doe."

The pillow was soft and inviting. Her eyelids gratefully closed—then suddenly opened again.

"Garrett!"

"What's wrong?" She heard the sound of his movements as he sat up, then stood. She could sense him starting toward her.

"Garrett, where was the pilot? What happened to the pilot of that plane?"

Silence.

"Garrett!" She began to be alarmed.

"You must have been the pilot, Laurie."

"Oh."

She could feel his presence in the dark. He was waiting. For what? Did he expect her to scream or dissolve into hysterical sobs?

Then she heard his voice from a distance. He must have returned to the couch. "You're the first pilot I've seen with such well-manicured nails." So that was why he'd inspected her fingers so thoroughly.

He said nothing more, and though she tried, she could not hold off weariness any longer. She'd think about things the next day.

She slept.

BUT MORNING SHED NO LIGHT on who she was or what had happened before Garrett found her. Opening her eyes, she lay very still. Any movement of her head brought a surge of the now familiar pain.

Sunlight streamed through the windows, concentrated in bright little islands on the floor. She remembered the previous day's events; they were still real and vivid. Slowly she pulled herself up to a sitting position, hugging the blankets in the chilly room, propping her back against the headboard. From the pain that shot through her, she guessed she probably had a broken rib.

There was no sign of Garrett, no way of telling whether he was still there.

Despite the pain, she edged out of bed and into the bathroom, where she splashed cold water on her bruised face.

Her face.

The mirror reflected a totally unfamiliar image. She stared, transfixed, renewing acquaintance with herself, searching for a key that would unlock the door to her past.

Her face might as well have been a stranger's. There was swelling on one side, and a tidy bandage on her temple was edged by a greenish-yellow bruise. The thick blond hair was tousled and badly in need of combing. Between discolored patches, her skin was smooth and clear and warm in tone. The eyelashes were dark, as were the well-arched brows.

"Ugh!" she exclaimed.

The medicine cabinet produced a tube of toothpaste, and she squeezed some on the tip of her tongue to freshen her mouth. She assumed there would be a toothbrush and makeup in her luggage—if she'd had any luggage and if it could be found. Surely no woman traveled without such vital necessities.

She examined the purple mark spread around her arm like a giant's handprint. Perhaps she had tried to protect herself and the arm had taken the brunt of the impact.

Sounds of movement in the main room told her Garrett had returned from wherever he'd gone. She limped to the bathroom door and saw him standing midway between the couch and the bed, a bewildered expression on his face.

"Good morning, Garrett Collier!" It was as though she were also saying, "See how well I remember yesterday."

"Good morning, Laurie." Relief softened his features, roughened his voice.

"Sleep did nothing for my memory," she confessed.

"Don't force it." The words were quiet, reassuring.

She changed the subject. "I'm searching for necessities such as a toothbrush and makeup."

"I have an extra toothbrush, and you don't need makeup."

"Flattery, and at such an early hour, too! Seriously, though, I looked in the mirror. I'm a mess!"

He regarded her almost proprietarily, stepping closer to survey her battered face. Then he picked up her arm and pushed back the sleeve, his finger gently brushing across the bruise. She stood patiently through the inspection.

"No one said survivors need be glamorous," he gently teased.

"Well, even makeup wouldn't do much for these cuts and bruises," she conceded. She paused before adding, "The real problem, though, is that I have no clothes."

The flannel pajamas she wore were much too large; she felt like a child playing dress up. She hitched up the trousers and headed, slowly, cautiously for the kitchen, an even more immediate reality—hunger—uppermost in her mind.

"Should you be walking?"

"I'll find out," she said.

Someone had spent time, effort and money in furnishing this mountain retreat, she thought as she made her way to the kitchen. Polished antiques blended gracefully with sleek, modern appliances.

His footsteps scuffed behind her on the tile floor. As she busied herself looking for pots and pans, she asked, "Do you like eggs for breakfast?"

"I'll just have toast today. But can you cook, Laurie?"

She paused, holding the frying pan in midair. "I suppose so."

She had been skimming along from minute to minute without thinking about what she could do and what she could not. Perhaps that was the way to get over the blank wall in her mind.

Just past the refrigerator was a rolltop desk and some radio equipment.

"Radio reception should be better today. The weather seems to have cleared." He gestured toward the alcove.

"Then I probably won't bother you for long," she commented.

His eyelids flickered. "No bother," he said, which had to be the ultimate understatement. "With snow twenty feet deep on the pass, there's no way out, anyway." The prospect didn't seem to upset him; perhaps he had played rescuer before.

"Garrett, what are *you* doing here?" she asked impulsively.

He put two slices of bread into the toaster.

"That's a long story. But I can assure you that I'm not hiding from the law, nor did I escape from a mental institution. Believe it or not, I have business interests here. And this house has been in my family for almost a hundred years, though of course, it's been modified from time to time."

"Lucky family," she observed.

"I am extremely lucky—in a number of ways," he said.

The coffee had finished brewing and she poured two cups, using only one hand; the other protected her rib cage.

"Don't you get lonely?" What had made her ask that?

"Not especially."

If he had come here to be alone, then she was an inconvenience, wasn't she? As he munched toast and drank coffee, he looked like nothing more than an attractive young man intent on enjoying his breakfast.

He looked up suddenly and caught her watching him. For a moment their eyes held, then she looked away. She tugged at the belt of her pajama trousers again as she shuffled to the counter to refill her coffee cup. When she turned to begin the slow walk back, he was looking at her, shaking his head.

He grinned. "First let's find you some proper clothes, since you insist on rising from the dead and rejoining the living. You can't do much in that outfit."

"I completely agree."

"My stuff won't fit, of course, because you're too small, but you're welcome to make alterations. Can you sew?"

Her shrug sent a stab of pain across her face. Garrett watched her anxiously, but offered no direct aid.

"I'll wing it," she said.

He grinned, white teeth flashing in his tanned face. "Sounds fine." His expression became thoughtful, almost somber. And it struck her with the force of a blow that he was an extremely attractive man. She felt an inner tremor.

"I'll continue calling you 'Laurie,'" he said inconsequentially.

She supposed that right now, it made little difference what he chose to call her. "That's not my name, of course," she said with assurance.

"But what if it were?"

She stared at him. Did he know more about her than he had revealed?

His face betrayed nothing; he certainly didn't look like a person hiding any secrets.

He had a way of conveying his private amusement. Not a smile exactly, more like a gentle easing of his mouth.

She polished off the toast, then pulled her hands up into the too long sleeves, "Look! I'm a scarecrow!"

He regarded her with strange intensity. "Hardly," he said fervently.

"I must have been wearing something," she pointed out, returning to the subject of her clothes. "When you found me, I mean."

"Blue jeans, red turtleneck sweater and pink down jacket."

"What happened to them?"

"Rather the worse for the episode, I'm afraid, although when they've been washed, they'll probably be decent enough. At present they're covered with dried blood and mud."

She suddenly realized how she must have got out of her soiled garments and into his warm pajamas. She couldn't help blushing at the thought that somewhere between the time he'd brought her into the cabin and when she'd awakened in his bed, he had completely undressed her. She felt the warmth rising in her cheeks.

"I'll launder them," she offered quickly, turning away.

"If I'd known you'd need them this soon, I'd have been more careful about getting them off." His playful tone lessened her embarrassment.

"You didn't cut them?" she asked, horrified. Her wish for properly fitting clothes became tremendously important as hope faded that any were available.

"I had to cut the sweater. I'm sorry."

As she rubbed the massive bruise on her arm and felt the twinge of the broken rib, she understood. "And the blue jeans?"

"They're only caked with red mud."

"I'll survive, then. May I borrow a shirt?"

"Certainly." He indicated the bureau drawer and the closet

As it turned out, she wore a pair of his jeans until she could wash her own. They were, of course, too large, but Garrett declared that with the red bandanna strung through the belt loops, she looked quite respectable. And it was an improvement on the loose-fitting pajamas.

He chuckled when she modeled the plaid shirt, which she had tied in front to take up the extra length.

"Not bad, not bad at all," he said. They were being very businesslike about solving her clothing problem.

He grew thoughtful. "You must have had luggage. I was so surprised at finding someone alive that everything except getting back here went right out of my mind."

"You did right, of course, but can't we go back and look?"

"What do you mean 'we'?" he took her hand and pushed up the baggy sleeve to expose the bruise. Somehow she knew he was thinking of her other injuries, as well.

She squirmed. Her rib wasn't bothering her as much now.

"I'm all right, really." She pulled her arm away.

She was not willing to acknowledge that his touch had an unusual effect on her. It was light and gentle, but at the same time compelling and possessive.

Nonsense, she thought briskly. But he made her uneasy in a way she didn't fully understand.

"Returning to the scene might help my memory," she suggested.

"Possibly. But not today. You're not strong enough yet," he said firmly.

He seemed determined to cosset her, and it wasn't an altogether unwelcome sensation.

He went to the radio, and she heard the click as he turned it on. He began to repeat call letters, but no one answered him; there was only static.

He worked at it for several minutes more, then shrugged and offered an explanation. "We're located in a pocket with notoriously bad radio and TV reception and transmission. And since this isn't the greatest radio equipment, it's doubly difficult to make contact. The static always clears up—in time." She sloughed off her vague suspicions as mere ingratitude. Surely Garrett Collier was exactly what he'd said he was.

By why was he here on the mountain all alone? Did her presence threaten his privacy? If it came to that, could she be sure her injuries had occurred in an air accident? The whole tale as he had told it sounded more like a mediocre movie plot. Suddenly she was not sure of anything.

She turned to the breathtaking view from the curtained window. It looked out on the white expanse sloping smoothly away from the cabin to where the dark green pines defined the curving limits of the meadow.

Midmorning, snow began to fall, softly and gently closing them in together. She puttered about, still nursing stiffness and aches but, all in all, feeling surprisingly well. She laundered the clothes Garrett had said were hers. Then she fixed them a soup and sandwich lunch, and they sat down together to the simple meal.

"You're a better than average cook," he said, grinning. They could pick up conversations where they'd left off, as though somehow privy to each other's thoughts. Neither seemed to notice this uncommon communication.

"Have you analyzed how you can recall activities such as cooking and sewing?" he asked casually.

"You sound like a therapist," she accused.

"Analyzing situations never hurt anyone," he defended.

"You're right," she conceded. "Actually, I'm trying to let events flow in and out of my mind." She paused. "I'm having trouble not worrying about what I can't remember." Tears suddenly rolled in great crystals down her cheeks.

She felt like such a fool, sitting there with her lunch in front of her, tears streaming down her face. He put her spoon down beside her soup bowl, then patted her shoulder awkwardly. "You're fine. There's no reason to be frightened. You'll remember, and when you do, you'll need to talk it all out."

Her tears ceased, dammed by a more immediate concern.

"Since no friends are present, I suppose that means you," she said waspishly. Did she want this stranger as her confidant?

"Beggars can't be choosers," he pointed out quietly.

But there were only two days' acquaintance between them, at least for her part. He had all the advantage; she was in his house, accepting his hospitality, wearing his clothes and eating his food.

After lunch he went to the coat closet, preparing to go outside.

She watched him in disbelief, glancing to the window, where the steadily falling snow formed a solid white barrier.

"Where are you going?" Where he went was none of her business, of course, but the weather looked so forbidding.

"I'll be back in an hour," he assured her. An hour! He could freeze to death in an hour.

He strapped on a pair of cross-country skis, whistled for the golden dog and disappeared behind the white gloom. She was alone.

When she could no longer see his form, she turned away from the window. The house seemed darker and emptier now. And colder. She crossed to the fireplace, poked at a smoldering log until it blazed into comforting flames.

It was no concern of hers if he wanted to go out in the blizzard and freeze to death, she fumed. She could get along. Of course she could. Straightening, she stood as erect as possible, assessing the pain in her lower rib cage.

Come on, Laurie, or whoever you are! You have things to do, she told herself. *As soon as the weather clears and your wounds heal, you'll make him take you to the wreckage.* Provided he even got back to the cabin. Surely they would find clues in the plane that would reveal where she had been going and what her name was, at the very least. But what if Garrett didn't make it back through this raging storm?

The snow continued, and she scolded him, wondering what would become of her if he never returned.

Twilight had already wrapped the house in gloom, when she at last heard him outside, talking to the dog. He was back! She flew toward the door, almost forgetting her aching muscles.

The door burst open, and the large golden dog pushed in and jumped up on her, slathering her face with wet kisses.

"Help! I don't need a bath, Winnie," she protested, laughing, protecting her ribs.

"She's a bit too affectionate at times," Garrett apologized.

"So I see—and feel." Wiping her cheek on her sleeve, she stroked the satiny golden coat.

"Thank you, Winnie, for saving my life," she said retreating to the couch.

The dog regarded her soberly, as though understanding every word perfectly. Then Winnie's nose came to rest in blissful worship on her knee.

Should she remind Garrett that she would have been left stranded and helpless if anything had happened to him that afternoon? There was no point. Here was here now.

"What's it like outside?" she asked.

"Cold."

"Aren't you clever? Besides that, I mean?" She gave him an exasperated look.

"Quiet. Beautiful."

"You're a man of few words."

He continued. "Awe inspiring. Dangerous."

"All right, all right! I asked a stupid question."

"Forgive my flippancy," he apologized. "I'm accustomed to solitude, after all, except for Winnie."

"And she never asks inane questions."

"Never." He stood in front of the bookshelf, pushed buttons on the stereo, and music flowed through the room, immediately making everything more comfortable and homelike.

"That's wonderful," she approved. "Why didn't I think of that?"

"What kind of music do you like?" he asked casually.

Again she was confronted with the blank wall in her mind. Again the feelings of frustration and aloneness surfaced.

"I don't know," she whispered, the moment suddenly grown dreary.

"I'm sorry!" his voice was stricken at causing her discomfort. "Don't think about remembering. Give the first answer that comes to mind."

"I'll try, but it's too late with music."

"Classical, jazz, rock, country and western—your choice," he prompted with a generous, sweeping movement of his arm.

"Can you arrange a mixture of all of the above, please?"

"Certainly, Laurie, whatever you desire." He bowed formally, comically diffusing her anxiety.

At dinner Winnie parked herself beneath the table at their feet.

"Cozy. She keeps one's feet warm."

He grinned. "Is she bothering you?"

"No, no. I'm perfectly all right now, except for a few aches and pains—and the wall."

He looked surprised. "Wall?"

She nodded. "The one in my mind hiding everything that happened before I woke up here. I still feel like I'm standing in front of a solid wall and can't see over or around or through it." She closed her hand into a tight fist.

Her eyes focused on a spot behind him. He watched in alarm, aware of her anguish, then covered her clenched hand with his own.

"Easy now. There's a door through that wall and we'll find it." His voice was gentle.

Her eyes finally came back to him.

"Finish your dinner, Laurie," he said quietly, still holding her hand.

She picked up her fork obediently. "I know I'm not Laurie."

"You're Laurie to me."

"Why do you call me that?"

He thought for a moment then began.

"You were breathing ever so slightly, but you were so . . . passive I felt I had to establish communication with you or you'd just . . . slip away. I was desperate. The name Laurie came into my mind, and I just kept calling you that and you seemed to respond. And the more I called you Laurie, the more I thought the name suited you. I know it doesn't make much sense, but that's what happened."

She realized then what a difficult task it must have been to bring her back to awareness. She could imagine the monumental effort he had made to detour her from the peaceful path toward death.

"It was close, wasn't it?" she asked, as if discussing a third person.

"My better judgment told me you were dead, that nothing would bring you back." His voice was low and she strained to hear.

"I owe you a debt I can't possibly repay," she said.

"If you never regain your memory, you may curse the day I revived you." He looked doubtful.

She shook her head. "Even if I never get past that wall, I'd rather be alive than . . ."

Now she was reassuring him he'd done the right thing. "I'm like a newborn baby, only I'm grown. My options are unlimited." She pretended cheerfulness.

But inside she wondered if she could cope with having her entire early life erased, gone as though it had never been.

He raised one eyebrow. "Do you always look on the bright side?"

She saw the significance of even such a simple observation. "I suppose I was like that before, too?" She raised her eyes, and was held by his watchful blue ones.

"I suspect so."

They were quiet then, savoring the dinner she had prepared when he was out, the dinner she had feared he might never return to eat. When he had finished his meal, he went to the cabinet at the end of the counter and took out a heavy green bottle.

He poured two glasses, handed her one.

"To the wall," he offered, the grooves at the corners of his mouth deepening.

"To the door in the wall," she replied.

"Correction." He smiled and drank, his eyes watching her through the glass.

The music wove gently around the soft cocoon of golden lamplight; the fireplace cast its half circle of warmth; the wine's effects began to spread through her.

"Thank you," she said.

"You're welcome." There was a short pause. "For what?"

"For being in the mountains. For hearing the plane. For going to look. For owning a dog. For calling me back from...wherever I was when it would have been easier to let me go."

He stared into his wineglass, his face still.

Then suddenly his expression changed, and he looked up, smiling broadly. "You're welcome, I'm sure. Drop in anytime!"

She threw a rolled napkin at him, which he caught deftly in his left hand.

"You're also expert at deflecting compliments," she said. "In any case," she went on, "since this is the maid's night out, you and I are responsible for disposing of the dirty dishes."

"Right. Shouldn't be too difficult. He got up and turned on the tap."

"And what does one do on long winter evenings in the heart of the Rocky Mountains?" she asked when the dishes were finished.

"I'll try the radio again, although it's not too reliable. I know I should have upgraded my equipment, but, then, my objective was to cut myself off from the world."

For almost twenty minutes he worked with the radio. She came and stood behind him, watching the gadgets and memorizing the call letters. Both of them were amazed when an answer came through at last. Her spirits soared and she clasped both hands together like a small child, her eyes shining.

Quickly Garrett relayed the pertinent information to the operator: aircraft description, location of the crash site. There was one survivor, a young woman, he told him, who was safe with him. He recited their latitude and longitude, as well as the exact mileage from Monarch, Colorado. By a quirk of bouncing airwaves, the ham operator Garrett had contacted was five hundred miles away in Kansas and would have to telephone the Colorado authorities. That sometimes happened with the great distances and the vagaries of radio reception and transmission.

Although radio communication had now been established, she realized that rescue would not be immediate. Miles of rugged mountain terrain still separated them from even the most rudimentary form of civilization. Half of that distance lay across a pass prone to avalanche, which any intelligent person would avoid. Garrett had chosen his hermitage well.

He turned from the radio, and she impulsively threw her arms around him.

"I'm found!" she exclaimed.

He hugged her gently in a long embrace, then slowly pushed her away.

"Careful, Laurie Smith Doe, I might not let you leave."

Was he serious? It would be easy enough; he'd only have to disable the radio so no one could confirm her location. She immediately dismissed the thought. Of course he hadn't meant it.

She felt like celebrating.

"Here's to your being found." Garrett reached for the wine bottle.

"Oh, yes! I feel like a party!"

He smiled. "With rather an exclusive guest list, I'm afraid."

"Well, I know more or less how I got to be a guest here." She paused deliberately, then said, "But you didn't really answer when I asked what you're doing up here, Garrett."

"I'm here on a whim, really," he said casually. Making it even more coincidental that he had been in exactly the right place when she'd needed him.

He went on. "I've been fortunate in business and in other aspects of my life. It seemed a good time to reassess my goals."

"I didn't intend to pry," she said. She sipped her wine, then walked to the fireplace. He soon followed and sat down on the couch. "What month is this?"

"November. Late November," he said.

"I wonder what I did on Halloween."

"Probably went trick-or-treating." He grinned.

"I wonder," she said thoughtfully.

"Christmas is coming. Do you want a new doll?" he teased.

"I don't think I'm a doll sort of person." Her mind searched for something solid to latch that idea to, any hint of what her childhood self had preferred.

Garrett watched as she struggled again to scale the blank wall.

"Except in appearance," he said gently.

"Do you think so?" She restrained herself from running to look in a mirror.

His tone was thoughtful. "My first impression was that you were a strictly ornamental item, so to speak. But there's the fact that you piloted the plane. You were alone. I confess I'm intrigued to find out just what kind of person you are."

That makes two of us, she thought.

"Are you certain there couldn't have been a pilot or another person you might have overlooked in your hurry?"

"I've wondered, too. I don't think so. No tracks led away from the plane, though they could have been covered over. But snow fell almost all night. A good thing for you, but fatal for someone trying to walk out. I believe Winnie would have alerted me if there had been another person anywhere in the vicinity. I'm almost positive there was no one else in the cabin itself."

"Garrett! Let's go back there!" She was too excited to sit still. "I'm all right now. I could handle skis or snowshoes, I know I could."

He looked at her speculatively, and she felt a strange breathlessness that had nothing to do with her injuries.

"In a few days." He sipped his wine. "We should hear from the ham operator tomorrow."

She found it impossible to settle down. Instead she paced between kitchen and fireplace, now and then taking a side trip to the bedroom area. An excited confusion of thoughts swirled in her head.

When at last she eased into bed she thought she would be unable to sleep, but as soon as her head hit the pillow she dozed off. The day had tired her more than she'd realized.

When she awoke the next morning, Garrett was already up.

"Hey, lazy no-account," he called when he heard her stirring.

She grinned, instantly awake, the past evening's discovery instantly returning. "Have you heard from the ham operator?" she called.

"The static is back." But that didn't seem to bother him.

"At least they know someone's alive over here. They'll figure out who I am." She shouted cheerful comments to him from the bathroom as she dressed and put her face and hair in order.

ALMOST A WEEK PASSED before Garrett judged her well enough to start out for the crash site. They had been unable to contact the ham operator again, nor had they heard from him. The quest for her identity was still on.

After breakfast Garrett pulled warm clothes and ski equipment from the closet for both of them, and they donned layers of coats and sweaters.

Once outside, she drank in the fresh brisk air. The inside warmth had been misleading and the winter air felt crunchingly cold. She had no difficulty fastening the ski bindings; she seemed to have almost a physical memory of the actions—she must have skied before.

For the first time she got a complete picture of the cabin's location. They were high, very high, nearly to timberline. The house sat on a little bump on the side of a good-sized mountain. Below lay a small valley, though from where she stood, she could not see if a stream ran through it. Across and directly in front another mountain towered, matching the ones on each side. Black against white, trees covered the slopes up to the clear-cut line where growth ceased. Off to the right were more mountains—they were like a child's drawing of interminable, inverted vees repeated on and on to infinity.

A sort of trail ran past the house, curving to a point where a wall of trees closed in, and she could not tell which direction it took from there.

Garrett knelt to check her bindings, and she felt an urge to touch the swirl of hair at the back of his neck, then caught herself with a start. He straightened, pulled his hat over his ears and passed two ski poles to her. Tentatively at first, she pushed one foot ahead of the other—with surprising ease.

Ever watchful, Winnie pranced and plowed beside her in the powder snow. They traveled at an angle to the slope's grade. When she fell back, the dog bounded toward her to offer encouraging yelps.

"Thanks, Winnie," she panted. After a few minutes Garrett stopped, waiting for her to catch up.

The trail climbed subtly, and it became necessary to pull harder and harder against the poles to propel herself up the slope. At first this was agonizing when bruised muscles strained against her ribs, but she found that it became less painful as she went along, although her arms tired quickly.

She stopped to look back. The little house was set picturesquely against the pines. Nowhere was there any other sign of human habitation. When she turned to follow Garrett again, he was close behind her; he'd apparently come back to reassure himself of her well-being.

"Oh, I'm not giving up!" she exclaimed. "I was just admiring the view."

"Sure." A smile stirred the corners of his mouth and she saw herself mirrored in his sunglasses.

He unzipped one of his jacket pockets and gave her a piece of chocolate. "For energy," he explained. She was grateful for the respite, and felt her flickering strength revive.

Cathedral-like stillness surrounded them, overwhelmed them with its vastness. When she spoke it was in a whisper. "This is so beautiful, Garrett. I can see why you'd want to stay all winter." He nodded.

They went on.

She found it tough going, though they rested often. She no longer accused Garrett of being oversolicitous but, on the contrary, was thankful for his thoughtfulness.

They came to a wooded area and threaded between tall trees, pushing aside branches that seemed to reach out for them. Winnie ranged ahead, circling first left, then right, occasionally tasting the snow. The dog's sense of duty periodically brought her back to where they toiled, to press her nose against them in anxiety for their welfare.

It felt as though they'd been traveling a long time, when Garrett pointed to a leaning pine at the edge of a clearing. "When I made it this far, I began to think we'd both make it," he said.

She memorized other scenes he described as milestones in their progress the day of the rescue, absorbing the information into her soul.

Something besides the high altitude made her heart beat faster. The cold and the snow and the smell of pines—were they all familiar, or did she just want them to be? She was not sure.

Garrett stayed close. Garrett—how could she ever thank him?

When they came abruptly into an irregular clearing he paused. Then he forged ahead, and Winnie yelped excitedly and circled around both of them.

"Garrett, she acts like she knows what we're looking for."

"She does," he replied. "Almost as soon as we headed up here she knew we were retracing the trail, so of course she expected us to wind up exactly where we found you."

"Dogs are amazing," she said. Was she babbling on about Winnie to quell her own fears?

Garrett led and she followed. The terrain was steep and they had to sidestep up the slope. Her legs were tired, and she didn't think she could go much farther.

A thick white blanket covered everything. There was nothing to suggest that anything unusual had ever happened in this place. Only a faint tracery of animal tracks disturbed the white smoothness, until Winnie galumphed across the clearing, plowing up snow as she went. The trees were true forest trees, their lower branches sparse, their upper branches forming a dense canopy high overhead. Boulders larger than houses were scattered throughout the clearing.

Winnie skidded to a stop, then began digging vigorously with her front paws, sending snow flying in a cloud behind her. Cocked head intent, she paused to glance at them several times.

"She's found something!" Janiver exclaimed.

"She's found the plane," came Garrett's monotone.

The dog dug frantically until she uncovered a patch of metal bright as blood against the stark white snow. Garrett stepped out of his skis, stuck them upright into the snow beside his poles and waded toward Winnie, calling softly.

Leaning against a jutting boulder, she undid her own skis, then jammed them into the snow. By that time, a larger patch of plane had been exposed, and Garrett was brushing aside the light powder to find the doorway.

She struggled up beside him as he pulled back a plastic sheet that covered an opening.

"Where did that come from?" she asked.

"I put it there when I requisitioned the door for a sled," he explained.

The effect of impact was evident. The seats had come loose and lay askew. Some of the gauges in the instrument panel were broken, and glass lay scattered on the floor. Miraculously the windshield was intact, but it was covered with snow and the sunlight filtered dimly through, casting an eerie light over everything. The upholstery looked old and inhospitable; it could as well have been that of an old long-abandoned plane.

"It looks like it's been here for years," she commented. This could not be what he said it was, could not be a plane that had recently crashed.

Ignoring her, he crawled inside, his hand touching a spot near the far window. "You hit your head here," he said. "The chrome right there is the same shape as the wound on your temple."

She regarded it with interest, then touched her head with cautious fingers.

"You could have hit the glass and gone through and there would have been no point in my coming up here at all." His mouth formed a grim line.

She ran her hands over the instrument panel, eyes closed.

"And I don't remember a thing," she said softly. She opened her eyes and gazed intently, searchingly into the rear of the tiny space.

Behind her he was quiet, waiting.

She put her hands on the controls, closed her eyes again and pushed. "This is how to go up," she said quietly.

Her hand reached out, fingers tracing the instruments.

This was a dream—something was happening. A young woman peered through a snow-covered windshield, talking desperately into a radio transmitter. The plane's nose pointed ever so slightly down, and the girl struggled to divert its death-bound course.

"Garrett!" she cried.

"Yes?"

He was beside her.

Her face was alight with revelation. "I remember!"

She turned to him, her expression a mixture of happiness and horror. "My name! Everything!"

CHAPTER THREE

"THANK GOD!" he said, cradling her in his arms, his large hand pressing her head into his shoulder. They clung in the crowded cockpit, tears streaming down their faces. They were laughing and crying at the same time, in mingled relief and shock and joy.

When she drew away from him her face was radiant, and the words came tumbling out.

"My name is Janiver Parmalee. I *was* piloting the plane. Flying is my hobby, but I model for a living. How could I possibly have forgotten?" She was incredulous.

Satisfaction glinted in his intense blue eyes as he looked down at her. The wetness on his cheeks did not detract from his masculinity.

His hands gripped her arms, loath to release her. "Very simply—everything was knocked out of you," he said. "You're alive by the grace of God and good fortune. You won the toss with fate."

She leaned against his broad chest in grateful support, weathering the shock of returning reality.

After a time they stirred, disengaged themselves from each other and crawled from the dark interior of the twisted wreckage. The snow-covered world smiled on them and Winnie bounced with joy and satisfaction at this turn of events.

Janiver patted the sleek, golden head. "Yes, you're a good dog. You did a marvelous job of digging up my plane once again. After this, we can let it rest in peace."

Garrett guided Janiver to a sunny spot beside a gray boulder, spreading his jacket for her to sit on. "Rest here. I'll get everything from the plane."

She leaned against the solid rock. "I remember packing. I was going to Steamboat to ski." She fairly bubbled with information, now that the wall had come down. Words poured from her as though it were her power of speech that had been stopped instead of her memory.

"You were headed for Steamboat Springs?" he asked.

"Why so surprised?" she said.

"You're two hundred miles off course."

She felt a momentary shiver of fear. What if she hadn't crashed in this particular spot? What if Garrett and Winnie hadn't found her?

He knelt beside her, watching her, his eyes again masked by the sunglasses.

"You never know," he muttered, shaking his head.

"What do you mean?" she demanded.

"I somehow expected that you'd turn out to be an hysterical female."

"Why, for heaven's sake?" she asked indignantly.

"You looked—" he hesitated "—fragile and..."

"And what?" She pursued.

He had a bewildered look on his face as he struggled to soften the words. "I don't know. I guess I assumed... I mean because of the way you looked..." Again he stopped.

She smiled at his obvious embarrassment, and at how wrong he had been. "Jumping to conclusions is rather illogical," she chided in mock solemnity.

She paused, then said, "I just thought of something."

"What?"

"I did a magazine ad last year for perfume—Laurel perfume." She stopped.

"Ah!"

"Did you see it?"

"I suppose I must have," he said slowly.

Suddenly everything made sense; all the pieces fell easily into place. She understood now why he'd thought of her as Laurie, why he'd felt that name somehow suited her. They eagerly worked out the details of their explanation, smiling in relief at his simplicity. Laurel...Laurie. The ad had been widely used—

was, in fact, still being used. Sometime during the past year he'd seen it, perhaps just glimpsed at it, but the name had stayed with him, subconsciously linked to that glossily perfect image of her face.

After a while Garrett ambled back to the wreckage, whistling a little tune. Janiver settled back, basking in the clear sunny day and the blessed ability to remember.

Memories crowded her mind like thousands of color slides. Her father, the ranch, Floyd, the agency. It was good to know!

She watched Garrett salvage her luggage and various usable objects from the fallen craft. He found a roll of canvas and spread it flat on the snow. He took a length of light cord from around his waist and threaded it though the grommets of the canvas.

Search planes would have passed over this clearing without a second glance. Parties on foot or on horseback would probably not have seen anything, either. Though the plane had undoubtedly sheared off some tree branches just before impact, any evidence was buried beneath the thick white mantle. Janiver shivered again at how close she had come to disappearing without a trace.

But she hadn't. She had only temporarily vanished from real life. The modeling agency must be wondering about her. There had been preliminary conversation about several upcoming assignments, and she hoped no one had replaced her. In modeling it was often a case of out of sight, out of mind. A career could go downhill very quickly.

Her father must be frantic. And Floyd. As soon as she and Garrett got back to the cabin they must try to contact the ham operator again.

And Allen! Allen Tobin! What about him?

Garrett methodically piled his findings on the tarpaulin. Her suitcase, her backpack, her downhill skis that she had brought for Steamboat, a first aid kit and other useful odds and ends he'd managed to recover from the plane. A newspaper.

Yes, she remembered that Floyd had placed the newspaper on the seat beside her, along with the two brown paper bags.

The sun had already begun to set when Garrett announced he was ready.

"I'll help," she offered eagerly.

"It's not necessary. I've put everything in the tarpaulin, which I can pull."

"Great idea!" Everything seemed wonderful when one had just emerged from the dark tunnel of amnesia.

Winnie led off and Garrett pulled the loaded tarpaulin as the little caravan left the clearing. Behind them was evidence of their activity: snow trampled about and twisted wreckage once more exposed. Their footprints blotted out the traces of animal tracks.

Garrett had wound the cord around himself so that the strength of his shoulders and upper arms bore the weight. He dug his ski poles into the snow, and the loaded tarpaulin followed smoothly after him.

Janiver straggled behind, her strength ebbing with the declining sun.

Garrett waited for her, politely pretending that he, too, was tired.

"Not much farther," he assured her. But she knew it wasn't true; they had only begun the return trip.

"I'm all right," she panted.

"Sure you are! You're perspiring, even in these arctic conditions. I'll leave the bundle until tomorrow and concentrate on getting you back."

"No. I really am all right. Let me rest just for a minute. I'll need my toothbrush!" Which, of course, was in the pack.

She stopped to lean against a tree trunk, closing her eyes. Just for a minute. Winnie nudged her hand, urging her to keep moving.

"Janiver!" Garrett towered over her, and she realized she had dozed off, also noted in detached surprise that she had slid right down into the snow at the base of the tree.

"I guess I am tired, after all," she murmured, her eyelids heavy.

"Get up, Janiver!" he commanded. "Now!"

She tried, but her legs were jelly.

"I never should have let you come!" he said harshly.

She wilted against him, her head on his shoulder. Holding her to him, he bent down, unfastened her skis with one hand and shoved them into the canvas-covered bundle.

"Janiver!"

She roused vaguely. "Hmm?"

"I can't get you home unless you help." His voice was severe and uncompromising.

"I will," she whispered obediently.

She opened her eyes to his face wavering above hers. A face roughened with concern. She wanted to tell him she would be all right, but no words came.

"I'm going to tie us together, but you must stay awake and you must put your hands behind my neck, tight! You have to!" he instructed sternly. "Do you understand?"

"Yes." Her voice trailed off drowsily.

He positioned her arms. Then supporting her, he crouched. She concentrated on keeping her hands locked behind his neck while he lashed rope around them both. When he had finished, she was positioned rather like a bedroll flung across his chest, with her face near his.

"Garrett . . ."

"Hang on!" He pulled himself upright with a grunt, then reached for his ski poles. She felt his muscles ripple as he pushed off, leaving the loaded tarpaulin behind.

After a few yards he paused to readjust the rope that held them together.

"You're slipping, Janiver. Hang on tighter!"

Her voice seemed to come from a great distance. "Yes, Garrett."

He shook her hard. "Open your eyes! Now!"

Her eyes were so heavy.

"Janiver, don't leave me!" It was a command.

Her eyes sprang open; his face looked gray in the deepening dusk. "I won't," she promised solemnly.

"Hold tight!"

She clenched her fingers. The pain that tugged at her consciousness kept her awake, kept her from slipping away from him.

Once more they moved on, and the chill air pressed ominously about them.

"Damn it, Janiver, if I have to talk you back again, I will."

What did that mean? She couldn't be sure of what she heard. Everything was dulled and confused by the fog clouding her brain. She'd have to ask him what he'd meant.

"Garrett?" she whispered, perplexed.

His voice cracked with anger. "I should never have let you talk me into going back. You're nowhere near well enough." The movement of his muscles was in rhythm with his words. Then she saw through the ruse—he was deliberately angering her.

"Why are you saying such awful things to me, Garrett?"

"You're awake, aren't you?" he asked grimly.

"Don't you like me?"

"You've caused me no end of trouble." The powerful arms knotted and then relaxed. "Don't let go!"

"I'm not!" She flung the words at him.

"Your arms are like wet noodles."

"I can't help it."

"You must help it, or we'll both die tonight."

Now it was almost dark and rapidly getting colder.

"Are we lost?" She couldn't believe that Garrett would ever lose his way.

"I stupidly forgot to leave a light on in the house. Any idiot knows better than that." His anger with himself stirred her into an effort of wakefulness.

"We'll make it," she comforted, fighting off a wave of unconsciousness.

"Garrett . . ." She went limp.

"Janiver!" His voice was edged with something she could not identify. "Stay with me!"

"I'm tired, so tired . . ." she murmured from within the drifting fog.

"Stay the hell awake until we get back to the house!" He sounded furious.

She was puzzled. "Why are you so angry?"

"Because I'm stupid."

"Where's Winnie?" she asked drowsily.

"Winnie!"

The dog gave a short yelp from the deep dusk beside them. Garrett paused, settling Janiver's body more comfortably against his.

"I can stand by myself," she murmured.

"No, you can't!"

"If you just hold on to me, wouldn't it be easier than carrying me?"

"Too late. We left your skis with the bundle of goodies."

She slid her arms from around his neck and rubbed them stiffly—it felt as though they were being torn from their sockets. He tightened the rope, pulling her firmly back against him. "I'm sorry if it hurts," he apologized. "I just don't see any other way."

They were again bound tightly together. He whistled for the dog. "Home, Winnie," he urged. "Show us the way home." In the gloom, the dog regarded him with ears cocked in a question.

"Home, Winnie! Take us home!" he urged again. The dog plowed ahead and Garrett followed. Janiver concentrated on her locked hands, fighting to keep them from pulling apart. On and on they went, until Garrett gave a sudden exclamation of relief.

"Thank God! This is our trail from this morning. Now if we're headed in the right direction, we might get home safely, after all."

The deepening cold knifed through Janiver's slender body. Despite his burden, Garrett moved steadily forward, crossing the snow in a smooth, practiced rhythm. Tentative little barks came through the darkness, guiding them on their way. Janiver's head rested on Garrett's shoulder, her face just beneath his ear.

"Hallelujah!" Garrett shouted.

But Janiver did not hear; she had lost consciousness. She was drifting once again through the familiar icy darkness.

When she finally opened her eyes, Garrett was standing above her, still clad in his outdoor clothes. She lay on his bed, the comforter tucked securely around her. She felt his hand pressing lightly on the inside of her wrist as he took her pulse.

From behind closed eyelids she heard him remove his jacket and sit down to tug off his heavy boots. Then she felt rough hands jerking the blanket away, unzipping her jacket. Her hair fell across the pillow when he pulled off her cap. She tried to tell him to leave her alone, but she could not push the words past her clenched lips.

His arm came around her and he raised her shoulders from the bed.

"Swallow this!" She obeyed his command, then coughed as brandy burned her throat.

"Garrett!" she sputtered.

"Sh!" He sounded amused and relieved.

"Just minutes ago you were giving me hell. Now you seem to be laughing at me. Just what are you doing?"

He grinned. "Trying everything I know to keep you from floating off into the great unknown."

"I keep having to be rescued, don't I?" she said with a sigh of frustration.

"You do have a flair for the dramatic," he agreed dryly.

She angrily clenched her hand, but he caught her fist and she relaxed.

"As long as Winnie and I are around, you'll be all right."

"But I got along very well before," she protested, surprised at the tenderness in his voice.

"Oh?"

"I really did. I'm independent as . . . as a cactus, and never need help."

"Well at least now you remember things like that about yourself."

"That's progress, anyway. Last time I woke up in your bed, I hadn't the vaguest idea who I was and how I got here."

He was smiling broadly again. "All women who wake up in my bed claim the same thing."

She regarded him gravely, eyes large and sober. She had not thought of other girls waking in his bed and wasn't at all sure she liked the idea.

"Winnie saved us both this time, didn't she?"

He nodded.

"Shall I help get something to eat?" she asked.

"Don't underestimate the management," he warned, shaking his finger in pretended sternness. "Give me a few minutes to whip up some food." And in not much more time than that, he created a very good meal. He carried two trays to her bedside, where they ate in companionable silence.

"You're wasted here by yourself, Garrett. You should be cooking for appreciative people," Janiver remarked as she finished her coffee.

"I'd make a good housewife?" he drawled.

"As a matter of fact, yes."

"Those are not really the words the average red-blooded American man wants to hear."

"How old are you, Garrett?"

"Thirty-one. How old are you Janiver?"

"Twenty-three. Oh, it's wonderful to be able to answer such a simple question!" She reached out both arms in an impulsive gesture of delight.

"I'm sure it is." He sounded as pleased as she was.

"When you call the ham operator, I have several messages."

"Of course." But the joy he'd shared with her had abated, though she really didn't understand why. He brusquely gathered the soiled dishes and carried them into the kitchen sink.

The deep chill in her bones had subsided after a cup of hot soup and another of coffee.

Now she felt a little like Pinocchio becoming a real person; first she tried one stiff leg, and to her surprise, she could move it normally. Then she carefully tested each arm in turn, and then her head and neck. And like Pinocchio, she was astonished to find that her whole body moved as she directed.

She heard Garrett at the radio, trying to send a message.

Laboriously Janiver swung her legs over the side of the bed and stood up. She flexed her fingers, which still ached from being locked so tightly together. Breathing deeply with the effort, she tottered to the kitchen, reaching the dining table before she even registered that Garrett was in the middle of a conversation with someone on the radio.

"For heaven's sake, man, don't bring a helicopter up here! The snow is too volatile. It would mean nothing but trouble!"

"But that is your correct position, isn't it, Collier?" a man's voice persisted.

"Yes, but I don't want any damned journalists causing an avalanche just for a damned news story!"

The voice replied. "I'll pass it on. Whether they'll come or not, I can't say. Just be prepared. Roger!"

Now Janiver stood directly behind Garrett, her hand lightly touching his shoulder.

"Who wants to do what?" she asked quietly.

"Channel 15 is all set to come rescue you in time for the six o'clock news," he grumbled.

"How do they even know I'm here?"

"The news is out, Janiver. The operator in Kansas got in touch with the Colorado authorities, and Channel 15 got hold of the information. They have their methods—and their reasons.

"Can they do that? Rescue me, I mean." The idea intrigued her.

"If they don't care whether they bring tons of snow and rocks crashing down."

"On us?"

"Probably."

"Tell them not to, then," she said recklessly.

"I did, but who can stop Art Herbert?"

The radio operator's voice interrupted them. "Any messages?"

"Oh, yes, several." Janiver took the microphone from Garrett's hand.

She gave the operator her father's name, then after some hesitation, Allen's, and his Steamboat Springs address.

As she recited Allen's name she felt Garrett stiffen.

"Anything else?" she asked over her shoulder.

He shrugged. "No."

She signed off and turned away from the panel of switches and dials. Something was obviously bothering Garrett, something that had been said before she got within earshot.

"What's wrong?" she asked, trying to make eye contact.

"Nothing." His face was shuttered and he refused to look at her.

"Coffee?" she inquired.

He nodded shortly.

"What was all that about Channel 15?" she asked when they had taken their coffee mugs to the chairs before the fire.

He stared into the flames, his face impassive, his thoughts unreadable. What had brought on this mood? He should be happy to be so close to getting her off his hands, and he'd never seemed moody before.

"That hotshot Art Herbert is going to use us to boost his show's ratings." He spoke reluctantly.

"I never watch Channel 15," she admitted.

"That's precisely why Herbert needs a sensational story. And he doesn't care whose privacy he invades to build his image."

"What's so sensational about Garrett Collier and Janiver Parmalee?" she asked curiously.

"When someone survives an airplane crash, that's sensational."

She nodded acknowledgment.

"You haven't heard of me, have you?" he asked, looking at her unbelievingly.

"Have I made a monumental faux pas?" Was he in films? Television? As far as she knew, she'd never heard his name or seen a picture of him. And she couldn't believe he was some notorious eccentric or a fugitive from justice. Why did he expect her to recognize him?

"No." His voice was gentle, though still doubtful. "I'm seldom recognized unless I want to be."

"That sounds mysterious and definitely 'poor little rich boy.'"

"And self-serving, too, I imagine." Then he apparently decided to set the record straight, once and for all. "I founded and am still the major stockholder in Technology, Inc., a company that dips into a great many activities."

"I have heard of that!" she exclaimed. "I thought some stodgy professor types were behind that."

"I am a professor," he revealed modestly.

He must think her the stupidest girl in North America. She resolved to start reading the business and science news more closely.

"And then there's my natural talent for sticking my foot in my mouth," she said wryly.

He grinned. "I don't see that my knowing your identity and your knowing mine should change things."

She said thoughtfully, "But it does, doesn't it? 'Wealthy entrepreneur' and 'fashion model' are quite different from 'mountain man' and 'mysterious blonde.'

"It all adds up to a story Channel 15 could do something with," he admitted.

She nodded. "Only Channel 15?"

"Channel 15 seems to have taken a special interest in your...adventure. This is exactly the kind of story Art Herbert is looking for," he said grimly. "But it's just a matter of time for the rest of them. When you get out the press will be waiting, and they'll ask you a zillion rude questions."

"I'm rather good at answering rude questions. I get those fairly often."

"I'm sure you do, but not about me."

She looked at him curiously. "You seem uncommonly concerned about yourself and your image in all of this. I didn't think you worried about such things."

His lips tightened.

"I was thinking of you, actually," he said, looking away. "It could be an inconvenience to be publicly linked to me—in any way. Especially by Art Herbert."

She raised her eyebrows. "I was beginning to think you were involved in drug trafficking or something," she joked. "And wanted this location kept secret."

"Nice that I've made such a positive impression on you," he answered dryly.

"But you've been outright secretive," she protested.

"I couldn't imagine you'd be interested in my experiments."

She was silent a moment, absorbing the unexpected—and yet unsurprising—information. "You mean you go out every day to check on experiments? Here in the mountains?"

He nodded.

"What kind of experiments?" she asked, adding, "perhaps you underestimate me."

He was looking at her differently now. "I may have at that. Obviously a woman pilot knows more than the average American female about weather and other scientific phenomena."

"Or the average American male." She couldn't resist the sly rejoinder as she demurely refilled their cups and set a plate of cookies on the low table. "So fess up, Mr. Collier, and stop underestimating the entire female species."

He laughed, throwing up his arms in an exaggerated gesture of defeat. "Okay, okay, I withdraw the remark. In any case, most of my experiments involve new products, and therefore aren't intended to be public information."

That went some way toward explaining his apparent secretiveness; Janiver was well aware that testing new products was usually confidential.

"Would Channel 15 interfere with your product development?"

"Possibly." He shrugged. "And I've tangled with Art Herbert before."

"I have caused you problems, haven't I?"

He shook his head. "Not really, though I suppose it would be simpler for me—and my experiments—if you were still lost to the world, at least until late February or early March." Was that regret in his voice?

"My swimsuit assignments come during the winter months."

"Swimsuits?" He sounded puzzled.

"At least I used to have swimsuit assignments.... I suppose it will be swimsuits with beach robes until the marks on my body are gone."

"The trials of modeling as a career!" he teased.

"A bit offbeat, isn't it?" She looked at him squarely.

Though their conversation flowed freely, she felt a change in him, an unfamiliar sense of restraint. What had he and the ham radio operator been talking about? Something had happened. Something she should know?

"Do you spend every winter here?" She was probing as delicately as she could for clues.

He shook his head. "This is my longest stay in years. It occurred to me that it would be interesting to see if I could live an entire winter all alone. Explore the physical and psychological aspects of living in isolation—I wanted to do it all and record it all."

"Like learning to swim by being thrown into the deep water?"

"You could compare it to that. But there's more. As I told you earlier, I'm working on several experiments monitoring new products and so forth." He paused for a long moment. "I don't want you to think I was lying to you the other night—I am here to reflect, to reconsider my life and goals. Everyone has to do that from time to time, and this was the right time for me. Fortunately the product testing and my personal experiment in solitude, so to speak, provided the perfect justification for retreating from the world for a while."

Silence stretched between them as they watched the flames licking the logs, methodically and steadily consuming the large pyramid of wood and twigs.

"That fireplace—" he gestured toward it "—is one of my experiments."

"How?" she asked, surprised. It looked like an ordinary fireplace to her.

He explained how certain features of the unit were vastly more efficient than most of the fireplace designs on the market.

"I hadn't noticed."

"Good! Then we can conclude that the average consumer will get as much psychological comfort and contentment from this version as from the drafty inefficient kind we all know and love."

She found herself genuinely interested in the merits of his innovative fireplace.

Suddenly he laughed. "You needn't give me that starry-eyed look, as though you're fascinated by what I'm saying."

"But I am!" she insisted.

He seemed doubtful and began to question her about her own work, listening to the answers as though he really cared. Suddenly he asked, "Who's Allen?"

"Allen Tobin," she said unhelpfully, taken aback by his abruptness.

He slapped a folded magazine against the coffee table in sharp frustration.

Janiver jumped, and her cup rattled. "Hey!" she protested.

"Sorry!"

There was silence again, awkward silence. Janiver watched him from beneath her lashes. His face was a study, but in what? Anger? At her? Well, soon enough he'd be rid of her. She obviously cramped his style and distracted him from his experiments.

And why should she explain Allen to Garrett? Allen was none of his concern.

She resolved that during the rest of her stay, she would take great pains not to get in his way or interfere with his projects. She set her lips firmly, drew a deep breath.

"Garrett . . ."

"Janiver . . ."

They spoke at once, then paused, each waiting too courteously for the other to speak first.

He laughed, a short mirthless burst of sound. "All right, I'll be rude and go first. Are you serious about this Allen what's-his-name?"

"No."

"But you were on your way to visit him?" he pursued relentlessly.

"That's true, I was." She paused to consider her answer. "But I was going primarily because all the reports said the powder was marvelous. And Allen said I could stay in his condo."

His frown deepened. "You were going to stay with him?" he demanded, his voice cutting.

"You make it sound so secretive and sneaky," she said resentfully.

"Sorry." He stared into his cup.

What was bothering him? The long silence weighed heavy on them both.

"How do you ever know who wins the important football games?" she asked, knowing full well that the diversion would annoy him because he wanted to hear more about Allen.

"What do you mean?" he asked impatiently.

"Do you ask the ham operators for the scores of the Rose Bowl game?"

"I presume you mean because of my isolation?"

"Yes."

"My ideas of what is important don't seem to be the same as those of a lot of people," he replied. "I get newspapers now and then, and magazines. I've discovered that the world doesn't stop if I don't know football scores."

Then, oddly, she wanted him to know all about Allen, how they had met and that their relationship was not special. She proceeded to tell him.

Garrett listened intently.

"So you see, he's only a friend," she finished.

"Why date him, then, if he's not special?"

"It sounds heartless, but I need someone to go around with. American life is not made for single women. Or single men, either, I suppose, though even after the feminist movement, it's easier for a man to dine alone, for instance, than for a woman."

"Do you often have to dine alone?" He was not looking at her.

"Frequently. When I'm on assignment with a photographer who is all hands and romantic notions, I have to plead something to get out of having dinner with him. Sometimes I say I'm sick, and then I go and eat candy and drink Cokes from vending machines. Sometimes I eat nothing at all—tell myself it's a diet."

"Now you sound like the 'poor lonesome career girl.'"

"I suppose I do."

"So you despise men with busy hands and romantic ideas?"

"I don't believe that's quite how I'd put it. I don't like a man putting the make on me for his own short-term pleasure."

"I would think you'd constitute a long-term pleasure, at the very least." He had finally turned to look directly at her.

"You know perfectly well what I mean. Quit being obtuse."

He let that go and smiled gently at her, signaling a change of topic. "Are you all right now?"

"Oh, yes. I feel fine. I thought I felt well enough to do grand things and make momentous expeditions, but when I actually got out in the cold and snow, I turned into a wet mop."

He chuckled. "Then I hereby declare you Prisoner of Shadow Mountain for another week."

She found that she didn't mind the thought at all.

This time he was the one to refill their coffee cups. "This will ruin my modeling career. I'll get fat and never be able to work again," she complained, reaching for a cookie.

"Haven't I heard about a new market for the larger woman?" he teased.

"That's not amusing," she said coldly.

"You obviously don't like jokes about your work. It seems to me there's another subject you're sensitive about. Each time I mention Allen, you start to talk about something else." His persistence in discussing Allen irritated her.

"Do I?" Perhaps he was right.

But if she was in love with Allen, she would be more likely to talk about him at great, boring length, wouldn't she?

"I'm not in love with him," she said, wondering where the conversation was going.

"But you would have stayed the weekend with him?"

She bristled. "Are you some kind of Puritan? Or perhaps the Commissar of Morals?" she asked stiffly. "Isn't it possible for a man and a woman to stay in the same house and not sleep in the same bed? I've been in your house longer than I was ever in Allen's, yet we haven't slept in the same bed—at least not at the same time." Her argument was becoming mired in confusion and embarrassment.

"True," he said after a pause that was longer than necessary.

She stood up abruptly. "Really, Garrett, I never thought you would be so..."

"So... what?"

"So... so insulting."

He stood, too, and they faced each other. The warmth from the fire—and from her unwanted display of emotion—had reddened her cheeks. "Insulting to think someone would want to sleep with you?" he asked pointedly.

She would not meet his eyes, hastily stooping, instead, to pick up the empty cups and plate.

"Janiver."

His hand captured hers. She looked up warily.

"Garrett, don't ruin things."

They stood like that, her hand engulfed in his; several times he seemed about to speak but said nothing. Then, without releasing her hand, he reached with his other hand to softly stroke her mouth, his fingers barely touching her lips.

She couldn't move.

"You'll soon be ready for the cameras again," he said gently, referring to her mouth, which had been swollen and bruised a few days earlier.

He confused her. From her first conscious breath in his house, he had been the epitome of kindness and concern, but now he'd implied none too politely that she was in the habit of sleeping around. And she found his actions of the past few minutes quite alarming. She didn't know what to think.

Protestations at his behavior would sound lame, indeed. Instead she adopted a distant dignity. She had, in fact, never slept with any man, had never wanted to. There had been times when she'd thought that perhaps she and Allen...possibly when they knew each other better... Now she was sure she never would. But why she was so positive on that point, she didn't know.

Things were different now, and it was because of Garrett. He'd saved her life; he seemed also to have changed her life—and she didn't know exactly how or even when that had happened. Still, she resented his prying into her emotions, resented his questions and insinuations. It was all so confusing!

Winnie, rousing herself from the hearthrug, glanced at them, annoyed, as though she took exception to having her peaceful slumber disturbed. Janiver knelt beside the dog, smoothing the golden coat.

"If she could, she'd purr," Garrett observed from behind her.

"Why don't you have a cat?" she asked. "You've thought of everything else."

"I had planned to, but at the last minute my five-year-old niece screeched at the thought of Uncle Garrett's taking away her cat, and my sister and I hadn't the heart to carry out the original plan."

The flames mesmerized her, warmed her with contentment. Soon she wouldn't have enough energy left to drag herself to bed.

"Any other relatives?" she asked.

"The usual set of parents, still married to each other after thirty-five years. The one sister I mentioned, complete with husband and the previously mentioned niece. One brother. The typical American family with slightly more than the average 2.5 children."

"My mother died three years ago, so there's only my father and me. Except for Floyd," she offered.

"Floyd?" His voice sharpened again. What was wrong now, she wondered irritably. His personality certainly seemed to be changing rapidly.

"Floyd Nolan. Friend, jack-of-all-trades at Dad's ranch. Not less than sixty-five years old and a wonderful, caring man."

"Not in Allen's category, I take it?" He released a breath he had held overlong.

"No, not at all."

"None of my business, anyway," he said lightly.

"True." But she kept her tone civil. Perhaps he was tired. After all, it must have been hard work, carrying her so far. He sat back on the couch, his long legs stretched toward the fire.

"I did thank you for saving me once more, didn't I?"

"Winnie saved us both. My stupidity almost got us this time, and just as you'd recovered your past, too." The dog stirred at the sound of her name, her tail thumping gently on the floor.

"Garrett, I think it might make an interesting news story if Channel 15 flew me off the mountain. I could mention your company in interviews and you'd get a bundle of free publicity." And she would be away from here—then she could stop worrying about making sense of all these unfamiliar feelings.

He shook his head. "Business is fine, thank you."

"Can Technology, Inc. really get along without you?"

"Are you implying that I'm indispensable?" His eyes twinkled with humor.

"Most company presidents are—or they think they are," she dared.

"I'm working on reducing the size of my ego."

"Really? My child psychology books said that basic personality traits are fully formed by age five."

"That's frightening, isn't it?"

She nodded. "But isn't it fascinating?"

"Tell me why you studied child psychology." He had turned attentively toward her, his half smile assuring her that he was interested in her answer.

"I had intended to be a teacher, but then modeling opened up, and frankly, the salary was far more appealing. I'll teach when I'm wrinkled and ugly."

"In other words, never?"

His indirect compliments left her feeling puzzled about how to respond.

"I'm not particularly good with words," he said. "Never have been much of a Casanova."

"I don't like Casanovas."

"Splendid!"

There, he'd done it again. If he had meant to, he couldn't have confused her more.

The day before she had been just Laurie, without a past, without family or career, without even a last name. Now she was Janiver Parmalee. In many ways, Janiver and Laurie were not the same person. Laurie had been born in Garrett's mind, born the moment he'd pulled her from that plane wreck and determined not to let her die. But Janiver Parmalee had a history, a childhood, a life that reached into the lives of other people.

Garrett had created Laurie, but Janiver Parmalee was a stranger to him. They had just met. Was it possible that he missed Laurie—or his idea of her? The thought intrigued Janiver, and she turned her head for a fuller look at him. He was slumped back, eyes fixed on nothing. He seemed tired.

"Garrett, do you miss Laurie?" The question burst out, and as soon as she spoke she realized how tactless it sounded. But she had to know.

He glanced at her apathetically. "Hmm?"

"Do you miss Laurie?"

He leaned forward. "There is no Laurie," he said bleakly.

Janiver rubbed Winnie's coat absently. "In a way there is. She's someone you created...." Her voice trailed off. She thought he wasn't going to answer.

He set his cup on the table, frowning, then intently brushed something from his sleeve. He was careful not to look at her. "I think you're right. I've felt somewhat hostile toward you ever since this afternoon. I could ignore my feelings on the way back because I was fighting weather and darkness. But after we got here, and things settled down and you were all right again—" He stopped.

Suddenly Janiver laughed. Winnie sat up on her haunches, obviously bewildered. After a minute Garrett smiled.

"Stop psychoanalyzing me," he protested.

"Hey!" she exclaimed. "Can't you see the headline now? Prominent Executive Falls for Figment of his Imagination."—

"Channel 15 would love it!" He slapped his knee.

Their laughter grew, forging a bond between them. Winnie turned her head from Janiver to Garrett and back again, an uncertain look in her soft brown eyes.

Still laughing, Janiver pulled herself to her knees, holding on to the couch for support. Her hand accidently brushed his knee as she reached for the armrest. His hand came swiftly down to cover hers.

"Janiver..."

Smoothly, naturally, his arms were around her, enfolding her. Unthinking, she let him raise her to her feet. Their faces were inches apart. His hand slid up her back to her nape and his lips met hers in a kiss. A kiss that demanded nothing, that promised everything.

They had been through a great deal together. Janiver had voyaged twice around a dark planet and come to rest here, in front of Garrett's warm fire. He had saved her from icy death, salvaged her from the wreckage. For what? For himself? When at last they drew apart, there was astonishment on both their faces.

"I didn't mean to do that," Garrett confessed, but it was not an apology.

Her gray eyes absorbed his face. "I know," she whispered.

And she did know. This was not a pass in any shabby sense of the word. The kiss had been spontaneous for both of them. A natural expression of—what?

Winnie took that instant to thrust her head between them and touch Garrett's hand, then Janiver's, with her cold, damp nose.

Garrett and Janiver stood there, his hands holding her elbows. The moment stretched on as though they could not bring themselves to break the contact.

Then he cleared his throat. "Time for Winnie's run," he said gruffly, then turned and strode toward the door. The dog trotted by his side, glancing anxiously up at him.

Janiver was rooted to the hearthrug. Could they go on as if nothing had happened? It wasn't possible. Because things were not the same, and it wasn't simply because the Laurie-Janiver business had been resolved. She shook her head. Right now, this minute, she would have welcomed any form of rescue, any way of escaping. She was suddenly overwhelmed by the strong conviction that this room, this house, harbored a threat, a threat to her freedom.

Garrett a threat? Ridiculous thought. He was probably less a threat than any man she'd ever met. Why, then, did she feel this urge to leave—and quickly?

She was still standing by the fire, staring into the flames, when she heard them come back in. She didn't look up as they walked past her.

"More coffee?" he called from the kitchen, exactly as if nothing had happened, as if nothing had changed between them.

"No, thank you."

Only then was it possible to put one foot in front of the other and walk the few steps to the bathroom door, to go inside and shut that door and lean against it wearily, as though she had come a long distance.

CHAPTER FOUR

SHE AWOKE TO THE SOUND of a typewriter, though she didn't immediately recognize it, because the staccato tapping had intruded into a dream about her father, Floyd and Winnie. In the dream the tapping became Winnie's toenails on the floor, and from behind closed lids Janiver waited for the inquiring black nose to suggest it was time she woke up.

Opening her eyes, she expected the dog to be standing by the bed. For a few more seconds, she hovered between reality and her dream. Winnie was nowhere in sight.

Patches of sunlight along the south side of the room were slanted, which indicated that it was close to noon.

She lifted her head from the pillow, surveying the room. The day before Janiver Parmalee had been reborn, and now, with the knowledge of who she was, memories swarmed about like mosquitoes. The experience had been a confusing one, and her mind was not quite ready to digest it all.

Garrett appeared around the corner, and she realized that the sound of the typewriter had ceased. What uncanny sense had told him she was awake?

"Good morning," he said carefully.

"Good morning." She felt shy; the kiss they'd shared the previous night had altered their relationship. He was no longer the mild protector she was used to, the man she trusted like a brother.

"I didn't mean to oversleep," she said, sitting up and hugging her knees.

"No problem." He was smiling. Strange that she had never noticed the shape of his mouth before. What would he look like without the beard?

"I take it the helicopter hasn't arrived, then?" she asked lightly, trying to keep the conversation casual.

"I've put them off for a little while. Sunshine and higher temperatures aren't helping your rescue. For that, we need two weeks of below-zero temperatures to stabilize the snow."

"Brrr," she said, shivering.

"There's no problem for us unless we're caught outside. Fortunately we're already been to the wreckage." He paused, "Do you still remember?"

So that was what worried him.

"Oh, yes. I'm still Janiver Parmalee and I know my address and everything little girls are expected to know. In fact, I'm beginning to remember some things I'd sooner forget."

He regarded her silently for so long that she shifted self-consciously. Did he intend to stand there while she climbed out of bed? Then what?

"Frankly, everything's been too confusing," she said hastily. "I feel like I'm on a merry-go-round." She stretched out her arms in a yawn, flinching at the tug of tender muscles.

He finally took her hints and returned to the living area.

She felt surprisingly fit after all the excitement of the past day. Twenty minutes later, washed and dressed, she came into the dining area.

Garrett was back in the study alcove, typing. He ignored her while she went about the business of preparing food. But when she made coffee for them both and brought him a fresh cup, he smiled briefly in thanks. Then he resumed his work.

She respected his concentration, and kept herself quietly occupied with a magazine, toast and coffee.

When she was clearing away her breakfast things, she found the paper bag of jewelry. She smiled broadly to herself, remembering their conversation. She now knew the plain gold band was not her wedding ring. The ring, earrings and necklaces were all purchases from a Denver antique shop. Janiver Parmalee remembered her collection of antique gold and silver in her bedroom at home. Floyd had helpfully loaded both paper bags for her. She could well imagine how upset he'd be if he knew the confusion his gesture had caused.

She whirled at the sound of Garrett's steps behind her.

"Garrett! Remember these?" She held out the handful of gold trinkets.

He stiffened. "More important, do you?"

"Yes. Yes, I do," And she laughed, amused again at how simple the truth usually was. "It so happens that I love antique jewelry, and had just bought this lot at a shop on South Broadway. And here we'd been making all kinds of assumptions about wedding rings." She paused. "Funny, though, Laurie didn't like the same things as Janiver."

His brooding silence drew her gaze up to his eyes, and her laughter faded.

"Janiver..."

"Yes?"

He looked away. "I had got used to Laurie, that's all."

A small smile played at her lips. "Janiver's nice, too. Really she is."

He gave her shoulder a playful swipe. "And it's nice that the bag contained a hobby rather than your family history."

"It was quite a dramatic touch, wasn't it? Now if I'd never got my memory back, what elaborate stories we could have created."

"Maybe we should write mysteries," he suggested.

"No need to invent fiction when you're living it. The greatest mystery is how to get me away from here."

"No rush."

"I'm losing money every day I don't work."

"And money is terribly important?"

"Well, yes, of course." She picked up the magazine from breakfast, leafed through to an automobile advertisement and held the pages toward him. "See?"

"Mmm." He inspected the layout carefully. "I didn't recognize you without your cougar."

"He's a pussycat—literally," she informed him.

Garrett took the magazine from her and stood there staring at the glossy photo as if he had never seen anything of the sort. It was one of her most prestigious jobs. A major auto manufacturer's newest production, with Janiver and the cougar dramatically draped across the hood.

"Is it difficult working with wild animals?" he asked at last.

She shrugged. She hadn't had any trouble with the cat; its trainer was highly skilled and the actual time spent close to the menacing claws had been short.

"You photograph very well," he continued, still studying the picture.

"Meaning I don't look that good in real life?" she teased."

"Meaning you're even more beautiful without cuts and bruises."

Her hand went automatically to her temple. "It's going away, isn't it?"

"Time heals all wounds."

"How profound. But I seem to have heard that wise thought somewhere before."

He grinned. "Fancy that!"

"I've always had trouble being properly respectful," she said, shaking her head in mock regret.

"You probably giggled all through your high school graduation ceremony."

"As a matter of fact, I did. And Girl Scout initiation, too." Despite the lightness of the conversation, she found his perceptiveness troublesome.

"You're lucky. It's all right for girls to giggle, but not boys."

"That's true. But don't you think women are entitled to a few small privileges? Men have every other advantage." She couldn't keep the note of sarcasm out of her voice.

"Is Janiver Parmalee a raging feminist?" His curiosity was aroused.

"I seldom rage, but certainly I believe women have had the worst of things for too long." She spoke seriously; it was important he know her feelings.

"On the other hand," he said, "sometimes women are their own worst enemies."

Was he baiting her? She looked at him.

"How many women executives are there at Technology, Inc.?"

"A few. But I confess that only a handful of our technical personnel are women," he said reluctantly.

"Why don't you hire more women?" She needed to understand his attitude toward women.

"For one thing, we get four times as many male applicants. Women go to college, get married and don't return to the job market until their education is out of date." Why did he sound so defensive?

"Who will care for the children, then?" she demanded.

"It is the dilemma of being a woman," he admitted.

"A true dilemma," she agreed. "Women can't win. We're criticized whatever we do."

"And criticism bothers you?"

He had a way of veering off a conversational path to gather up tidbits of her thoughts and feelings. By now she saw through his tactics, though heaven knew what she had already revealed. No other man had ever really cared how she felt. Most had been too interested in her exterior to pause long enough to ask about the inner Janiver Parmalee.

"What were you writing?" she asked. If he could detour the conversation, so could she.

"The black binders on that shelf are product logs. I record any observations that might be useful."

He was as thorough as any person she had ever met, yet he wasn't the least bit stuffy. With that conclusion, she decided it was time to end this bout of conversational detours and exploratory expeditions into each other's minds.

So she set about convincing Garrett that she needed fresh air and was fit enough to go out. After the previous day's experience, he wasn't likely to accept her word without a battle.

"No!" he exclaimed as she put on her down jacket.

"I'm all right, Garrett. I need fresh air."

His face still forbade her to go.

"I'll have Winnie," she coaxed. And he relented.

A short time later she and Winnie set off down the trail. Janiver's legs felt strong again. By some miracle she had survived two crises—with help from Garrett Collier.

Suddenly she felt a lump of icy wet snow being thrust down her neck. She gasped and turned to see a grinning Garrett, aiming more of the same ammunition directly at her face.

"Garrett!" she shrieked. "Stop it this minute!" Her protests echoed down the slope and back up again as he chased her with handfuls of snow. Winnie added to the din by barking eagerly, begging to be included in their game.

Janiver scooped up some snow, threw it at Garrett. He leaned down for a new supply and she ran forward quickly, pushing him over into a drift. Before she could escape, he quickly reached behind his back to grab her leg, and she fell on top of him.

"Such a fighter!" he commented, trying to ward off her hands as she struck out at him.

"That was mean, Garrett!" she panted, pushing snow at him as fast as she could, her arms working like propellers.

Their bodies rolled and twisted on the snow. His strong arms failed to deflect the small avalanche she created, and he was laughing too hard to protect himself effectively. Finally, in a coup de grace, she shoved an icy handful inside his collar where his shirt was unbuttoned and the short dark hairs showed.

At that he swarmed up, overwhelming her and pinning her against the snowbank. Her hat came off and her hair spilled across the snow in a golden shower. She fought him seriously, as though he were a genuine threat, as though this were a real struggle.

But it wasn't long before his strength was victorious and he forced her arms to her sides.

"Give up?"

She shook her head violently.

His laughter vanished and his face became very still. "You're a beautiful woman," he commented quietly, quickly releasing her and rising to his feet, stretching out a hand to pull her up. Her eyes glittered, and exhilarated by the tussle, she looked ready to resume the battle.

He put one finger under her chin. "Janiver, wouldn't you rather stay here with me than go work for a living?"

She was breathing deeply, her chest heaving from exertion. "Garrett, you're joking," she said breathlessly. She couldn't read his expression.

He was silent a moment. Then he smiled gently. "You could cook and do my laundry."

"How generous of you!" Her tone was scathing.

"Even career women have husbands they take care of."

"I didn't understand you were proposing marriage," she said slowly.

There was a pause.

"You could hire on as housekeeper. That's the position open at the moment." Oh, he was a careful one, wasn't he?

"No, thank you! I prefer the career I've worked hard to build." She drew away from him.

Playfulness had fled, and they walked back to the house, their faces bright with exercise and cold—and something else.

"I hope you're not a male chauvinist, Garrett," she said.

"Traditional roles are traditional for valid reasons," he replied carefully.

"You're being rather cryptic, but I suppose you're going to say the traditional division of work makes sense."

He nodded.

"I know all that. But it's damned depressing not to be appreciated, to be constantly taken for granted. If a woman gives of herself and her labor freely, it's love and that's great. But she's got to choose to do it, and that choice has to be valued by the people she loves. Otherwise, cooking and sewing and having babies becomes joyless—and borders on slavery."

His expression was inscrutable. "I wouldn't want you bound by slavery, of course." He hesitated. "I think I understand, Janiver. But . . . you can't quite know how very comfortable it is to have a woman in the house. And I don't just mean someone to make breakfast and bring coffee—though that's great, too."

Oh, yes, she thought wryly, the best of all possible worlds, what every man wanted and felt he deserved. Coffee and comfort. She hoped Garrett had heard what she was saying.

That night she lay awake a long time, thinking. Wondering what he had meant about not going home. Wondering what home would be like when she got there. Thinking of their conversation. Most of all, thinking about the fight in the snow and the glorious feeling of his touch. There was too much pleasure in being touched by Garrett Collier, even in the occasional slight brushing of his hand when she gave him his coffee. To say nothing of the other times when he had held her and caressed her. Yet she really did not know him. He was still a stranger.

It was time she left Shadow Mountain.

She must find a way to leave, even if it ultimately meant accepting the Channel 15 helicopter. Staying here would be a mistake. No, she couldn't stay. Tomorrow she would call Allen.

Allen. She painstakingly built his image in her mind, held it tight. But Garrett's face came and replaced Allen's. She turned impatiently in the bed so that she faced the window, where moonlight filtered through the blind. Finally, exhausted, she slept.

THE NEXT DAY was exactly what Garrett had said they needed—clear snapping cold.

She was preparing lunch and he was fiddling with the radio. He was supposed to be calling Allen, but he didn't seem to be having much success. That didn't surprise her; where Allen was involved, Garrett reacted halfheartedly at best.

"Garrett, where do you live?" she suddenly asked. "When you're not living here, I mean."

He laughed. "Where would you guess? Do I seem the high rise type, for instance?"

She shook her head. "I went to a party at one of those luxury high rise condos last summer. Most of the men I met who lived in the building seemed very much impressed with their own talents." Not like Garrett at all, she thought.

"And you, being honest little Janiver Parmalee, did you tell them the emperor was wearing no clothes?"

She turned to look at him. His allusion to her distaste for sham astonished her. How could he know she hated being around people who pretended to be something they were not?

"I—" she stammered.

He smiled at her across the room. "Didn't you know I knew?" he asked.

She turned back to her mixing bowl. "No," she said. "I didn't think anyone knew."

"Why keep your feelings a secret?"

"You can't imagine what a handicap it is to be introduced to someone famous and know instantly that they're as phony as play money. It's...uncomfortable. Because I can't say what I feel, but I can't be completely honest and sincere and all those admirable things, either. That's another reason I'm not very social."

"What's the first reason?"

There he was, prying again. He already knew enough.

"Aren't you going to answer?" he nudged.

"The other reason is that I'm tired of men trying to pick me up," she blurted.

"And of course they do." His voice vibrated like a taut bowstring.

"Yes." She nodded and poured the results of her studious mixing into a baking pan, then put the pan in the oven.

"Here's Allen," Garrett called from the radio.

"Hi, honey!" The voice, distorted a little by the airwaves, was Allen's, all right.

"Hi, Allen. Sorry to miss the skiing." Janiver was intensely conscious of Garrett's presence.

"The powder is still here, deep and delightful. As soon as we get you out of that place, you can come over." He made it sound as though she were stuck in a pit somewhere—or a prison.

"This place, Allen, is fantastic, and Garrett has been wonderful."

"Garrett?"

"Mr. Collier."

"Oh, yes." There was a pause. "*The* Garrett Collier?" She glanced over her shoulder. There was a strange glint in Garrett's eyes, and he gave a slight, noncommittal shrug.

"Yes," she told Allen, looking straight at Garrett.

The pause at the other end stretched too long.

"Just the two of you?"

"Well, there's a great golden dog named Winnie," she said jokingly, but Allen wasn't laughing.

"You were lucky, Jan."

"I know. Lucky that Garrett happened to go looking for the plane."

Another pause.

"Tell me about it when I see you," Allen suggested.

"When will that be?"

"I've had some conversations with Channel 15 and Art Herbert."

"Please not that way, Allen. I'm sure in a few days we can ski across the pass and someone can meet me at Monarch."

"Why the objections to the helicopter? It would be faster—and fun."

"Garrett says the snow is too unstable and the vibrations could start a bad slide."

"Are you safe?"

"Oh, yes. The cabin sits well out of the path of any slides."

"But you can't see any city lights from there, eh?"

"Most definitely not."

"Can we talk at the same time tomorrow? Be good, Janiver."

"Weather and airwaves permitting. Bye, Allen."

She automatically shut off the radio.

"You know your way around a radio shack, don't you?" asked the voice at her shoulder.

"Oh, I'm sorry! Did you want to talk more?"

"No. You're the one they were interested in."

"They? Was someone there besides Allen?"

"I think so."

"What makes you think so?" Allen wouldn't exploit his acquaintance with her—would he?

"Something that was said at the very first. Someone else was there when I made the first contact."

"The ham operator?"

"No, I don't think so."

What questions had Allen asked? She tried to remember exactly how the conversation had gone. He had asked who was in the house besides her and Garrett. That fact alone could make headlines, she supposed. The possibilities of innuendo were limitless. She didn't want a career that was accelerated by notoriety. Fame was one thing; that was earned. But sensationalism she found distasteful.

Unfortunately contact with the outside world had only muddled an already complicated situation. Garrett had been right; they should have let well enough alone and played Swiss Family Robinson until the winter was over. But it was too late now.

Both were quiet and reflective as they sat down to lunch in a subdued mood.

"You're a good cook, Janiver."

"Thank you." How courteous he was. It wasn't the type of calculated courtesy some men affected to impress a woman, but courtesy that was a natural part of his character. She couldn't deny it; he was exceptionally good company.

Yet here he was, as isolated from the world as he could contrive. She ventured the question that she had yearned to ask for some time now.

"Do people ever call you eccentric?"

He reacted in mock horror, answering in a comic cowboy accent. "Shucks, ma'am, no one never called me a nut, at least not to my face."

She ignored his attempt to distract her with humor. "Seriously, Garrett. What do people think?"

"That's the least of my worries." He calmly continued eating.

What was he like in his Denver office? Did he wear a three-piece suit, she wondered. He would look very handsome dressed up, she decided. What kind of house did he live in? He had not answered her exploratory probe about where he lived.

If this cabin was anything to go by, she felt his other home would be extremely comfortable.

Who were his friends? She wanted to know everything about him. She was about to launch her inquisition, when he spoke.

"I'm me, Garrett Collier. I'm fortunate to be able to do what interests me, rather than fulfill an obligation to some employer for the sake of an average living."

"It's not all luck, of course."

"Not completely. My parents helped a great deal—in encouragement when money wasn't available."

"Did you grow up in Denver?"

He nodded. "One of a minority—a genuine Colorado native."

"Where did you go to college?"

"Stanford."

Her eyebrows rose in appreciation. "That's not easy," she said.

"Who needs easy?" He smiled.

She felt she was beginning to know this man. He was kind, thoughtful, courteous, decisive, wise…. The words that sprang to her mind were so flattering that she shifted uneasily. *Careful,* she told herself, *no one's perfect, not even Garrett Collier.* She resolutely set aside the subject. She did not need to discover any more good points about him—not right now.

Garrett had retrieved the abandoned pack the previous day, and now she had her makeup kit. In the afternoon she indulged in a beauty binge of nail polishing and a facial.

The day wore on; she felt comfortable and content. Garrett wrote busily at his desk. She scarcely realized how intensely aware she was of the other person in the cabin and his movements.

She inspected herself in the bathroom mirror. She stared hard at her face; signs of the accident were fading. There remained a three-cornered red mark near her right temple, but she could comb her hair over it. If she was posing for windy scenes they would just have to be photographed from the opposite profile. She didn't think the accident would spoil her chances for good assignments. That is, if she ever got back to Denver.

She pushed up her sleeve and examined the bruises, which had faded to greenish yellow. She had pulled the shirt from the belt of her jeans and was checking her rib cage, when she suddenly heard Garrett's voice beside her. She looked up, startled, to see him leaning against the open bathroom door.

"What are you doing?" he asked. "Is something wrong?"

She hastily straightened her clothes. "I was looking for permanent scars," she said quickly.

"Are there any?" He ignored her confusion as he drank from the coffee mug in his hand.

"A few, but I think I can hide them."

"What if your face had been badly disfigured?" He might have been taking a scientific survey, for the lack of emotion in his voice.

"I suppose I could have had plastic surgery." But she didn't want to think about it.

"I mean—" he was impatient "—who *are* you without beauty?"

The question took her by surprise.

"I presume that's some sort of compliment."

"You know you're beautiful. The emperor might not wear any clothes, but Janiver Parmalee is a beautiful woman."

What would she have done if her face had been damaged beyond repair?

"I don't borrow trouble, either," she chided.

"How wise you are." They stood close to each other, unwilling to let time move forward.

"How about a ski run down the road?" he said, changing the subject.

"Super!"

The exercise felt good and the thin sharp air brightened her cheeks to a healthy pink.

The profound stillness of the little valley reminded her of a great, vaulted church. They moved through it in silent awe, leaving their parallel trails behind them.

The sun had passed the midpoint of its journey toward the west. Janiver knew that she and Garrett were heading slightly southwest, but without help from the sun's position, it would have been easy to become disoriented. Now she understood the usefulness of the horizon; navigating in the mountains was not so different from navigating in the air.

The powder that had fallen several days earlier had settled, and she had no difficulty keeping up with Garrett, although she knew he was not going at top speed.

It had been two weeks since the accident. A few changes in the course of events and she would have been lying dead, probably still undiscovered, in the dark twisted wreckage of her plane.

She shivered, but not from cold. Winnie chose that moment to drop back and run beside her, looking up at her in reassurance.

They reached the point where the road plunged into the forest. Garrett executed a graceful turn on his skis and Janiver imitated the move. Through a gap in the trees she could see the gray-red boulders, spotlighted by a shaft of sunlight. She gazed around her in leisurely delight. The winter-bare branches of aspens were like antique silver filigree, she thought, or Victorian lace doilies.

"This must be gorgeous in summer, too," she said.

He nodded. "Yes, but unfortunately, most summers I only get up here for a few weekends.

"The house seems awfully permanent for a summer home."

"We usually have caretakers, but they're spending the winter in Arizona."

She gave him a quizzical look. "What interesting people you associate with—caretakers who take the winters off."

He laughed. "I guess I do at that." They stood awhile longer, watching as the retreating sun lengthened the shadows and painted purple hollows among the peaks.

"Had enough?" He slanted a look at her.

She nodded and they started for the house, just visible in the distance. It, too, was changed by the sun and shadows, and now blended into the scene of grays and blacks and purples.

Janiver had to work very hard at getting herself back up the deceptively gentle slope. "Where are your experiments?" she managed when they were on the relatively easy homestretch.

"Why don't you come with me sometime? They're scattered about the mountain and valley, each located in the most strategic spot for the particular experiment."

"I'd love to come."

As they reached the cabin she said, "Have I spoiled your winter, Garrett? Would you have rather been alone? Am I the unwelcome variable in your experiments?"

"Hey! You're talking my language! Where did you learn about constants and variables?"

She laughed. "I went to college, too."

"I didn't mean to be condescending," he apologized, taking off his skis and leaning them against the cabin. Then he knelt to unfasten hers.

"I can do that," she protested.

"But you needn't." She let him take care of her.

When they'd stowed the equipment, they stood waiting for the sun to set, a round orange ball balancing on the rim of the mountain. Here were no glorious red or pink clouds. In less than a minute the source of the earth's light simply vanished, without fanfare or tantalizing display, a straightforward exit. Warmth was gone just as quickly, and the evening chill edged them inside.

"The outing was marvelous!" she said impulsively. "I needed that."

He crossed to the fireplace and added a log. At the same time he checked a gauge beside the heating unit and wrote in a note pad he took from his shirt pocket. No doubt their round of exercise had been part of his research, too, she thought. Did he ever relax? Or was he always the scholar, always observing the causes and effects of a situation with scientific objectivity? Nice as he was and considerate as he was of her comfort and wants, wouldn't that kind of life get frightfully monotonous after a while? Not that she planned to be here much longer.

She handed him a mug of hot chocolate.

"I suppose the only way to cross the pass is on skis?" she asked.

He sipped the hot chocolate, giving her a shrewd look over the rim of the cup.

"I can probably clear the road without too much trouble."

"It was sunny today."

"Yes."

"So do you think there's a possibility?" she prodded.

"Don't be in such a hurry. Or haven't you done your Christmas shopping?"

"As a matter of fact, I haven't. This is a nice vacation, but I do have a life to get back to."

"Your health has almost returned to normal." He was being the scientist again.

"Yes, I think so. Our little trip today was invigorating, but not tiring. Not like when we went to the plane."

"Hardly. This time at least, you made it back under your own power."

Again she was reminded that she owed him her life—twice.

He stood looking into the cheerful flames. "I'll see that you get to Denver. But you must allow me to proceed in the way I judge to be best for all concerned—you and the rescue party." And best for him? she wondered.

"I didn't mean to be a nag. I trust your judgment."

"You seem rather impatient."

"Yes, I suppose I am. You'll have to help me keep my feet planted on solid ground."

"Don't worry, I will," he promised.

And that more or less ended that.

He put on some quiet music, then scanned the bookcases, pulled a volume from a lower shelf and settled down to study.

Janiver riffled through the magazines in the rack and then searched out a book for herself. Soon she was deeply engrossed in a mystery novel.

Much later, she closed the book, then stretched and rubbed her eyes. She would take a shower and shampoo her hair. As she walked past Garrett, he glanced up.

"How about a sandwich?" he asked.

"Mmm, that sounds good. I was going to wash my hair."

"I'll make sandwiches while you do your hair."

He seemed comfortable with a woman in the house. Was it simply because he had a sister? Or was it something he'd learned from a wife? Or perhaps from live-in friends? Would she be prying if she asked?

"That sounds great."

She gathered shampoo and towels and went into the bathroom, emerging twenty minutes later with her head swathed turban fashion, her face completely free of makeup.

A plate of sandwiches was set on the table and he had brewed coffee.

"Garrett," she said. "There's a flaw in your Eden."

"Something serious, I'm sure," though he didn't seem worried.

"You don't have a hair dryer! That's the worst possible omission when entertaining overnight women guests." She reached for a sandwich. "Mine should have been in my suitcase, but I may have forgot it at Dad's."

His forehead was creased. "I suppose Allen Tobin has hair dryers for women who stay overnight at his place?"

Heedlessly she ran on, "He probably has, but I can't confirm it. I've never stayed there."

"I thought you had." He pounced on her statement like a cat on a mouse.

"What gave you that idea?"

"You did."

"Mr. Collier, what kind of girl do you think I am?" She pretended to be deeply shocked, melodramatically raising her hand to cover her eyes.

"You needn't go quite so strong on the wronged maiden role," he said dryly.

"Do you really think I sleep with men of short acquaintance?" Not that it was any business of his. Nor were his opinions, one way or another, any concern of hers.

"Most women do."

"I'm not most women."

"No, you're definitely not."

"Sometimes, Garrett, you say the most ambiguous things, and I don't know how to interpret them."

"It's not important."

Yes, it is, she thought, but let it drop.

She towel-dried her hair, allowing her robe to fall loose in the process. She moved closer to the fire and knelt on the rug before the flames, turning her head from side to side to catch the warmth. She ran her hands absently through her long, honey-colored hair, holding up strands to dry them in the fire's heat, letting them drift back onto her shoulders.

Exactly when she became aware of Garrett's gaze on her, she was not sure. She glanced around, then turned quickly away. His expression as he watched her was full of longing, naked and intense, and it disconcerted her. She had seen that look before, on the faces of other men. She had thought Garrett was different.

But she knew he had the same needs and desires as any man; she also knew, instinctively, that he would be a gently passionate lover.

Flames licked at the pine log, industriously reducing it to ashes. Her hair was nearly dry.

Then he was beside her with a steaming cup of coffee. She hadn't heard him leave.

"Why so thoughtful, Janiver?"

"This is a thoughtful sort of place."

"It is, isn't it? A major advantage when one has thinking to do."

"Where would I be if you hadn't wanted to spend the winter thinking?"

That anxious look crossed his face, the same expression that came each time she mentioned her accident. Earlier she'd wondered if it was fear, but now she understood that whatever he was, he was seldom fearful.

"We both know where you would be," he said quietly.

"There aren't any other houses for miles?"

"None this side of the pass that are occupied in winter."

"I don't know how I could have missed seeing that storm coming." Her sense of failure showed in the droop of her shoulders. "Or at least made more of an effort to get a decent weather report."

"Mountain weather forecasting is never a sure thing," he comforted. "I hope to have a few improvements for weather

forecasters soon. Some of my people are doing preliminary research now, and reliability has recently moved up on my priority list.''

He had done it again—made the kind of comment she suspected was a compliment, delivered in his most objective, scientific, impersonal manner.

''I would like to be as committed to my work and have my
future planned as well as you,'' she said.

''You don't like uncertainty,'' he suggested, and once again
she felt he'd read her character accurately.

''I like working, and I can always find something to do, but
it seems so much more exciting to have specific goals to pursue.''

''Setting goals and having the means to pursue them is the
best of all possible worlds?'' He had raised his eyebrows at his
own question.

''Yes.''

''But there are some things lacking even in my best of all
possible worlds.'' He sounded almost grim.

At the tip of her tongue were poised the words: *Because
you're all alone in the world. If there were someone sharing
it . . .*

But for all she knew, someone did share his world. Janiver
was still not certain whether there was a woman in his life. He
knew how to treat women; he was at ease with women. This
house and this valley constituted only one segment of Garrett
Collier's life. In the city he headed his own company, owned
another house. His life there was no doubt quite different from
the way it was here. She knew nothing of that—and never
would.

She rose abruptly, hugged the robe around her and tied the
belt tighter; her hair swung freely down her back like a golden
waterfall.

She could not stay here. Not with her increasingly mixed
feelings toward Garrett, not with Allen hinting half-truths to
the world.

Allen had not sounded like the Allen she thought she knew.
Or had this experience made her a stranger to herself? She had

to find out, had to leave this house, this valley, this man—Garrett Collier.

Feet dragging, she walked slowly to the bedroom.

She felt so confused, as though her emotions were all at war within her. There was shame at failing as a pilot, at not succeeding in the flight across the mountains. She still didn't understand how she could have made such a serious mistake. There were her feelings about Allen; they had changed since she'd come to Shadow Mountain. There were her feelings about her career. The prospect of far-off shooting engagements had lost some of their allure. Why?

There were her feelings for Garrett, unacknowledged feelings like dormant flower bulbs, feelings that with care and culture might grow and bloom.

She shut the bathroom door sharply and reached for flannel shirt and jeans. Perhaps the robe she wore was a bit suggestive.

"And God forbid I should be suggestive!" she stormed, surprised at her own unreasonable anger.

When she was dressed, she braided her hair in one long plait, marched out, randomly grabbed a book from the shelf and curled up in a corner of the couch. She had been staring at the opening page for several minutes before she realized she was holding the book upside down. She stole a hasty look around and decided that Garrett could not possibly have noticed. She quickly turned the book around and willed herself to concentrate on page after page, but it might as well have been written in Greek.

CHAPTER FIVE

THE DAY LOOKED GLOOMY from the very beginning. When Janiver opened her eyes, she thought at first it was still night. Although the shortest day of the year was not far off, the light reflected by the expanse of snow outside normally made the inside of the cabin quite bright from morning until late afternoon.

She snuggled under the comforter, feeling lazy and lethargic, unable to summon the energy to get out of bed. She was bored.

She and Garrett were too different in interests and personality. He was too absorbed in his work. She had played housewife; she had admired the arctic beauty around them. She had read extensively from Garrett's library—and admittedly learned a great deal, even though his literary choices were not necessarily hers. But now she was at loose ends. Whatever there was to do, she perversely did not want to do.

When she could, she studied him surreptitiously. With his broad shoulders and muscular arms, clad in jeans and flannel shirt, he could have been a lumberjack.

In the past few days she had come to realize that she wouldn't mind his making love to her. Reluctantly she admitted that she was physically attracted to him and that she couldn't help responding to his nearness. When by chance he touched her, she couldn't look at him, afraid of what he might read in her eyes.

But she wanted him to touch her. And she wanted to touch him in return. She'd never felt this way about Allen or any other man.

But Garrett made no untoward gestures—to her bewildered annoyance. He'd been the perfect gentleman. The cozy, friendly

relationship they had shared was now a polite chill. They were
courteous with each other, too courteous. The joking and
bantering were gone, gone perhaps with the kiss in front of the
fire, or the time she'd seen the longing in his face, the yearning
look she recognized from other men, the look that was simply
lust. Garrett's innate courtesy was all that kept the emotion
decent.

Garrett was not other men; he was himself. Just as Janiver
was herself, quite immune to outside pressures. Perhaps they
were too independent, too strong for compromise.

She had to get away, get home. She remembered the previous day's conversation with her father, when they had talked
about just that. He'd complained that reporters were dogging
him and Floyd almost constantly. "Jan, you can't believe the
questions they ask," he'd said.

"What do they say?" she had asked. "There's nothing to
hide."

He'd refused to be specific, and from that Janiver inferred
the reporters had cast slurs on her morality.

"Dad, what are they trying to get you to say?"

"Never mind," he'd said. "They're manufacturing a front
page story."

Garrett had been across the room and, she hoped, had not
heard the conversation. "Dad, is Garrett Collier that well-
known?" she had asked.

"Jan, if you read the business section of the newspapers
regularly, you'd have recognized the name immediately."

"But I still don't see any reason for scandal."

"Honey, it's not a scandal exactly. It started as an heroic
rescue. I guess things are a little slow in the news business, and
reporters have good imaginations. Nearly every day there's a
reminder that you and Garrett are still stranded on the mountain together, usually followed by some subtle speculations on
what you're doing. They claim they've tried to contact you,
with no success, and then they embroider the tale some more.
I tell you, Jan, it's a full-blown sensation. And of course they
run pictures of you both all the time." He chuckled. "I must
say you make a nice-looking couple."

"Dad!" she'd sputtered in embarrassment. "How could . . . you know that I— Oh! Listen, the next time, just tell them I said I was bored. That should kill some of the rumors."

"I'll do that."

"Tell them I can't find my hair dryer, and then they'll know I'm bored."

"Good idea," he'd said with a laugh.

"And Garrett can give you the name of a special date of his and they can all chase her for a while."

"There's no name to give them." Garrett had spoken from directly behind her.

She'd jumped, not realizing he'd come over to stand so close. "Oh, sorry, Garrett. Can't you make one up? Just to give the paparazzi something to get them off Dad's back?"

A smile had spread slowly across his face. "Tell them I'm going to marry Laurie Smith," he'd said distinctly.

Janiver had continued with the conversation, keeping one eye on Garrett, trying to interpret his statement. "Dad, did you get that?"

"Yes. Laurie Smith. Where does she live?"

"Let them ferret that out themselves," Garrett had said grimly.

"Bye, Dad."

She'd signed off, then turned from the radio, a mischievous grin on her face. "Laurie Smith, huh?"

"Did you like that?"

"It was an inspiration. We should have thought of it before." They had talked pleasantly for the rest of that day.

Now, lying in bed with the comforter warmly bunched around her, she laughed delightedly at the recollection, reveling in the poetic justice of Garrett's ruse. Sending the reporters after Laurie Smith—what a perfect idea!

Still contemplating that very satisfying memory, she sat up, then sighed as she looked around the room. She crawled out of bed, not looking forward to beginning the day. Another day of feeling bored and restless. Another day of not getting too close to him. Another day of polite, inconsequential conversation.

"Good morning, Janiver."

He was already at the breakfast table.

"Good morning."

"Why don't you come out with me today?"

She yawned. "I might as well."

"Try to control your enthusiasm," he commented dryly.

"Sorry. Garrett, I don't see how you can stand a whole winter here by yourself," she burst out.

"With you to cheer me up, it's no effort at all," he said sarcastically.

"I can't even pretend to be cheerful, not today."

"Today just started. Give it a fair chance," he counseled.

The prospect of adventure helped. Quickly she dressed in layers of warm clothes before gulping down her breakfast.

"How cold is it?" she inquired between mouthfuls of toast.

"So cold that Rudolf's nose would turn blue," he said.

"Ha!" she muttered.

Three-quarters of an hour later they were off, with Garrett leading the way.

The sun stood a few degrees over the eastern peaks. In the meadow a lone tree cast a shadow longer than the tree was tall. The vast silence was awesome.

They moved swiftly across the pristine whiteness. As they dropped down the hill, the house was lost from sight. They came to a small fold of the mountainside where boulders jutted through the snow to form a protected semicircle.

He stopped, removed one glove. She waited several yards behind, wondering whether she should be an indifferent observer or push closer and ask every question that came to mind. She decided that she would listen to any information he offered about the tests he was running, but she would not make the first move.

In a few minutes he was back at her side. And as she'd hoped, he concisely and matter-of-factly explained what he'd been doing. He described how he was monitoring the effects of mountain weather on an experimental kind of insulating material. Then he paused and said, "It's beautiful here, isn't it?"

"It's gorgeous. Can this world be part of the other one?" she asked almost philosophically. Which world was real? This one that looked like a Christmas card and felt like a cathedral? Or the one that included her job, her family and rushing here and there to meet deadlines, to make a living?

"Maybe this is the real world." His face was turned to the sun, soaking up warmth.

"Speaking of . . ." she began.

"Let's not, not now."

He pushed ahead and she followed. The next site was in deep shade beyond the edge of the forest, a spot that probably never felt the sun's direct rays, even in summer.

And so the morning went. Garrett led her from place to place, giving her a brief explanation of each experiment; most of them had to do with conserving energy and using it more efficiently. They traveled in a large circle that brought them back to their own front porch.

She was exhausted; she was exhilarated. She had been fascinated. "Thank you, Garrett, that was fun!" she exclaimed as she shed skis and layers of clothes.

His slow smile flashed through his brown beard. "Really?" She could not read his eyes behind the reflecting goggles. Didn't he believe her?

"Oh, yes! It was even better than taking a run with Winnie, though that's good, too."

The closing door shut out the brilliant white world. Shut the two of them in together.

"Hungry?"

"I could eat a bear," he said.

"Are there bears up here?"

"No problem," he said, grinning. "They sleep all winter, remember?"

"Have you seen any?"

"Not for years."

"I wouldn't like to meet one."

"They'd be more frightened of you, unless you bothered their cubs," he reassured.

While they talked, she was assembling a meal, making coffee.

Even before they'd finished lunch, someone was trying to reach them by radio. Garrett slowly walked over to the instrument panel to respond. After a moment he turned to her, saying, "It's for you."

Rather shamefaced, Janiver sat down in front of the set. "Yes?"

"Miss Parmalee?" The voice paused. "This is Art Herbert, Channel 15 in Denver."

"Good afternoon," she said courteously.

"How are you today?" The voice was just a little too hearty to be sincere.

"Fine," she fenced.

"I have fantastic news!" the perfectly modulated voice continued.

Janiver glanced behind her. Garrett stood like a statue between her and the lunch table.

"I've been concerned since you became stranded on Shadow Mountain, since your plane disappeared."

She murmured something about his kindness but realized he was listening to himself rather than to her.

"I now have permission to take you off Shadow Mountain by helicopter."

"But I'm sure my father has the situation well in hand," she protested.

"Oh, we're working with him. Make no mistake, this is a cooperative effort," he quickly assured her.

So this was it. The moment she had waited for. Her opportunity to get off Shadow Mountain. And away from Garrett Collier. Away from the mixed-up way he made her feel, sometimes high, sometimes low, sometimes as though she didn't exist, sometimes as though she were the center of his universe.

On the outer fringe of her field of vision, Garrett still stood. Waiting. For what?

"Miss Parmalee?" The deep voice reminded on a note of perfectly calculated concern.

"Yes. Yes, I'm here. I—I'm overwhelmed.

"How are you and Collier getting on?"

Ah, now she understood. The real object of his curiosity was Garrett, not Janiver Parmalee. The wealthy aloof business-man was Art Herbert's true target. She supposed that a suc-cessful man who went his own way would always be news worthy.

How should she answer? If she paused too long, Herbert could create quite a scandal from her silence. If she spoke in too enthusiastic a tone, he might also find significance there. Her heart beat faster, like a small cornered animal's. "Mr. Collier has been extremely kind," she said cautiously. Behind her she heard Garrett let out a long breath.

"I'm sure he has," the liquid voice insinuated.

She must not rise to the bait. Art Herbert wanted her on the defensive so he could imply there was a need to be defensive.

He tried again. "For my viewers' benefit, can you describe what it's like on Shadow Mountain?"

"Mr. Collier has a comfortable place here, well equipped for all emergencies."

"Prepared for staying all winter?"

"Certainly."

"Do you want to stay until spring?"

She'd made a mistake. "Not at all, Mr. Herbert," she cor-rected smoothly. "You must have misunderstood. I'm thank-ful events occurred as they did. Without G—Mr. Collier, I'd be dead."

"That's putting it bluntly, Miss Parmalee," Herbert said. "What is your reaction to surviving such a close call?"

Again she paused. "I thought I'd answered that, sir. It's difficult to condense into a few words. I shall never again take life for granted, no matter what goes wrong. I shall never say a prayer that does not include thanks to Mr. Collier for saving my life." She drew a deep breath. Had she overstated? Had she said anything that could be twisted into an embarrassing situation for Garrett?

But the deep voice surged on excitedly. "I believe I have a plan of action that will result in successfully getting you out aboard the Channel 15 helicopter. Here are the details—"

Garrett interrupted, his hand on her shoulder. "Just a minute, Art. Collier here. I strongly advise against coming directly here or doing anything so foolish as landing the chopper in my front yard. The snow is ten to fifteen feet deep and extremely unstable. A helicopter's vibration could touch off a massive slide."

"Hello, Garrett." The jocular familiarity surprised Janiver. Of course. Garrett told her they were acquainted. But the conversation was far from friendly. As the men exchanged ideas, it was as though each stood in the other's path. Garrett was cool, objecting to anything Art Herbert suggested. And Herbert resisted Garrett's proposals.

Garrett seemed not to want her to leave. Or was there a serious threat that a helicopter could cause an avalanche?

She listened as the two sparred and jockeyed for position. Finally they compromised. Depending on the weather, Art Herbert would contact them again in the next week. He was not giving up his chance at an exclusive interview with Janiver. Not yet. Weather permitting, Janiver and Garrett would ski to the pass. At the same time snowplows would be clearing the road from the other side. They'd meet on the pass, and that was where Channel 15 would pick Janiver up, either by helicopter or four-wheel drive, whichever was appropriate.

When Art Herbert signed off, Janiver and Garrett stood looking at each other, aware that the arrangements signaled the beginning of the end. This interlude was almost over. It had been pleasant enough, even taking into account her boredom—or whatever it was that made her feel so discontented.

Of course she wanted to leave. She had a million things to attend to—her career for one thing. And her flying; it was vital that she climb into a cockpit again and prove herself a competent pilot. She could hardly wait to be off Shadow Mountain!

Then why wasn't she happy?

She shook her head. Shadow Mountain was a mere stopover, a way station on the trail back to civilization. Back from the plane crash, back from darkness.

This room was a vastly comfortable place to wait out the interim, and Garrett was a vastly civilized man. The few times she had thought he was becoming too familiar, too intimate, he had drawn back—almost to her regret.

She ventured, shyly, to glance at him, and saw a strange expression on his face. She turned away again, wondering if the look on her face reflected his. Until now, the idea that she would eventually leave Shadow Mountain had not seemed quite real to them.

"Progress at last!" he said too loudly.

"Yes." Her own sounded shrill. "It's a good plan, awfully practical. How long a run are we contemplating from here to the pass?"

"About thirty miles, as the crow flies. It should be smooth going until we get to the slide area. I doubt if we can ski over that, unless there's new snow. We'll have to wait and see." Unemotionally he laid out his plans to her—plans that would mark the end of her stay on Shadow Mountain.

"Nothing to it." Her voice was as brittle as frozen taffy.

He seemed oblivious to the churning emotions inside her.

"How can I help?" she asked.

"First, let's put the whole plan on paper so we don't forget anything. That way we won't make the same mistake we made when we went back to the wreckage—not leaving a light on almost killed us." She didn't dwell on that sobering thought.

As Garrett got a blank sheet of paper from his desk and began listing the provisions they'd need to take, she heard him cursing under his breath. Something about Art Herbert. She decided it was time to find out exactly what was going on here; she was beginning to feel like a pawn in a game.

"Don't you get along with the man from Channel 15?" she asked carefully.

He hesitated. "I suppose you have a right to know. Art Herbert and I go back a long way. We've had personal differences—and philosophical ones." He paused. "Back in our college days, Art was interested in a girl who turned out to be interested in me. He's always resented me for that, though I certainly did nothing to encourage the girl. Cindy, her name was. Later he worked for me in public relations, but I had to fire him. We had serious disagreements about his PR strategies, which I considered questionable at best. Art took the job with Channel 15 soon after. So there you have it. Art Herbert is a man who holds on to a grudge. He's also a man who'll do anything for a story, even it if means twisting the truth."

Janiver felt stirrings of concern and guilt; her arrival had disturbed Garrett's way of life here, and her departure was going to upset things, too.

Later, when she talked with Allen, her mood had changed.

"I'll be getting out soon!" she told him.

"Great! How?"

She related the tentative arrangements.

"Ah!" he said. "I talked with Art Herbert a few days ago. Guess he finally saw things my way. What a scoop this will be for him!" Something about Allen's response wasn't right, and a chill swept through Janiver.

"Please, Allen. Dad and Art Herbert have things in hand. You needn't worry about anything. Mr. Collier and I can handle the details now. Thanks for your help."

"I'll be waiting on Shadow Mountain Pass, Jan. It's been a long time."

He seemed a mite too eager to share the spotlight of her homecoming, but she thrust her misgivings away as unfair.

Across the room Garrett looked up with a scowl. He opened his mouth, then pressed his lips tightly together, as if forcing words back down his throat. She knew that Garrett and Allen would not get along at all.

The next days were occupied with accumulating the equipment needed for their excursion. "Garrett," she asked at one point. "We can't stay out overnight! Where will we stay? You said yourself there aren't any other houses this side of the pass. We'll freeze!"

"There are some abandoned cabins that might do for shelter, or we could build a cave of snow."

Her eyes grew enormous at the thought. "Really? How?"

"There's a book about it on the shelf," he indicated with a nod.

"I should have known. You think of everything, don't you?"

"Yes, ma'am!" He raised his hand in mock military salute. "I aim to please."

Now that they knew she would be leaving, the tension between them relaxed. Once again it was as though they were sharing a unique adventure, the way it had been during the Laurie days. There was a spirit of cooperation, a common goal, though now that goal was Janiver's departure.

One night she glanced through the book about snow caves and decided it sounded practical, though difficult. But whatever happened, if she was with Garrett, things would be all right.

She tried to avoid thinking of the moment when she would step from Garrett's world into the other one. Allen had promised to be there, waiting at the pass. Channel 15 would be there, taking credit for the rescue. There would be interviews and countless questions, and doubtless, more insinuations. And when that was all over... what?

Time sped by as they geared up for the grueling trek ahead of them. There were the daily cross-country outings, practice for the real thing. At those times the weather varied from snow to sunshine, but they stayed inside only if Garrett considered the weather to be actually dangerous. As they trained and planned for the coming journey, the days seemed to fly by. It was already the middle of December. Garrett warned that after the first of January they could expect even heavier snow, weeks on end when the pass would be blocked. They would have to leave soon.

Winnie sensed the coming separation, and stayed close to Janiver's side.

Garrett said they should ski the rounds of his experiments with loaded packs, to become accustomed to the added weight. That went very well and Janiver did not tire too much. Nevertheless she resented the fact that Garrett's pack held more than hers.

"Garrett, I can do it! I can carry my fair share. I'm tired of being looked after."

"Janiver," he growled, "it makes more sense for my pack to be heavier—you're recovering from serious injuries.

"I'm better!" she snapped.

"No need to be upset." He calmly adjusted the packs.

"I'm not upset!" she protested. "But I'm not a hothouse flower, either."

She saw the beginning of a smile on his face and a glint in his eyes when he turned to her. "No, you're certainly not the kind of person I thought you'd be when I first saw you."

"Such a long time ago," she said thoughtfully.

"Not so long." There was a stillness in him.

"You've never said what you require in payment for my rescue." She held her breath. Did that sound as though she were fishing for future commitment?

His mouth curved in a soft smile. "We'll discuss it over dinner some evening in Denver."

She tried to hide the gladness she felt sweeping across her face. He wanted to see her!

"When will you be back?" It seemed vitally important to know when she would see him again.

"The end of April, possibly a little earlier."

April! He might as well have said doomsday.

She had become used to Garrett. Despite her chafing at the confinement, she really did not mind being here. But she did have her career to consider, and she missed her father. And sometimes she felt a craving for the company of others, for crowds and bright lights and the busyness of the city.

As the last day approached, they discovered a reservoir of things that had to be said now—or left unsaid for months. They talked almost nonstop from morning until late at night; they talked freely about everything—the whimsical and insignificant as well as more serious matters. They exchanged opinions and confided fears and told each other secrets.

One thing they talked about was flying, whether Janiver would be frightened when she again entered a cockpit. He thought not; she wasn't so sure.

"Were you ever afraid of flying?" he asked.

"No. Except..."

"Well?"

"Just before the crash I was terribly frightened." She shivered and felt again the sense of failure that came whenever she thought about the crash.

"I suspect it's like falling off a bicycle and climbing on again," he assured her.

"A combination of self-disgust and shame?" she asked.

"Exactly."

She took heart from his faith in her.

"I would like to be there when you go up again," he said wistfully. It was the first time he had indicated that he would no longer feel completely satisfied with being alone.

"Don't tell me you fly, too?" She wouldn't be surprised.

"No, I don't. But I'm going to learn as soon as I have time for lessons. I just mean . . . I guess I wouldn't be much help to you, would I?" He seemed astonished to encounter something he could not shield her from.

"That's what I've been saying to you for days and days now. Some things I must do for myself," she exclaimed.

"You're right," he conceded, though he sounded disappointed.

It was sweet of him to be concerned. Sweet. Garrett was sweet.

In the business world where he controlled the lives of hundreds of people, she doubted if anyone called him "sweet." The scientists who read his articles in learned journals might say Garrett Collier was thorough or innovative or any number of other things—but never "sweet."

She, too, wished he could be with her when she flew again. But that was impossible. He would be here in the mountains.

They practiced weather forecasting. Garrett taught her what to expect when the clouds looked a certain way at sundown. It went a bit further than the nursery rhyme, "Red sky at night, sailor's delight." But folk sayings often contained more than just a grain of truth, Janiver reflected one evening.

On Wednesday the official forecast predicted clear weather for the coming weekend. Highway crews would start clearing the road the next day and, in all probability, complete the task by that Saturday.

"It sounds like the night I left for Steamboat," Janiver commented cynically.

"Let's give science the benefit of the doubt," Garrett said. "Especially when the only other weather vane we have is our own senses."

He was right, of course.

In the late afternoon, he went to stand on the small porch, assessing the weather. She watched him covertly, dawdling as close to the doorway as she dared, anxious to know what he thought.

He stood bareheaded, practically sniffing the outside air. Involuntarily she gave a little sniff herself, and he heard her and turned.

"I'm wondering whether or not I agree with the official forecast," he explained.

She went to stand beside him. To her surprise, she found that she could actually smell something more than the familiar scent of pines and cold. The sky was a soft velvet gray where the sun had disappeared, and there were stars in the east. The evening air gently brushed her cheeks like the merest breath.

Time was growing short. Everything was ready. That night they made radio contact with Denver, and all the arrangements were confirmed. Friday they would leave for the pass.

She woke early on Thursday and immediately remembered that this would be their last full day together.

Garrett treated it like any other day. His experiments and observations held first priority, and he wrote in his notebook and typed entries as if nothing had changed.

Janiver searched the pantry for the makings of their last dinner. As she pulled packages out of the freezer, she grumbled to herself that he probably wouldn't even miss her cooking. Although he had generously turned that task over to her, he himself was an excellent chef. But, then, he was expert at everything he did.

The next day she would leave; she would leave this charming snowbound prison to go back to her father and Floyd—and Allen.

The agency would be calling. Or was Janiver's face already forgotten? She had been out of sight for several weeks now, and in the fickle world of fashion, it didn't take a long absence for a model to be put on the shelf.

The next day they would strap on their backpacks and skis and start down the trail that would lead her back home. It was too soon, she thought in sudden panic. She wasn't ready. Couldn't she stay a few days longer in this warm cocoon? Away from newspaper and TV people, away from reporters who asked embarrassing questions.

She added red wine to the prime cut of meat for the oven, set the timer. She didn't know what to do with herself after that. There seemed no point in beginning any new projects, since she wouldn't be able to finish them.

She turned on music, softly, so as not to disturb Garrett; she leafed through a magazine that she had perused countless times before. After a while, she got up and paced restlessly. Her movements were constantly followed by Winnie's puzzled brown eyes as she lay in her usual place on the hearthrug.

Janiver stood looking out the window, down the hill and across the open space where Garrett had said elk came to feed in spring and fall. He'd told her they had all gone to lower altitudes to escape the deep snow, and that as the snow melted they would return. But Janiver wouldn't be there.

The sky was gray, but not threatening. She liked it better when the sun shone, creating diamonds on the snow. She turned abruptly, almost colliding with Garrett. Startled, she gave a little scream, then raised her eyes to his face.

His hands steadied her, stayed on her arms.

"I was just thinking." she explained, not taking her eyes from his. Sometimes he seemed to know her thoughts. Did he now? His face was grim, his eyes blank.

Suddenly his smile bloomed, and his arms returned to his sides and he took a step backward. "You're going to miss me?" he suggested.

She hesitated. "I think I will, Garrett. You've been..."

"Yes?" He was teasing; he had no intention of letting their parting become maudlin. She almost wished he were more sentimental, though at the same time she silently thanked him for making things easy.

The afternoon finally ended and evening crept down to surround the cabin. Lights from the windows formed rectangles on the snow.

Their last evening together.

The table was formally laid, with wineglasses by each plate and crisp linen napkins and even candles. Music played quietly in the background. When they sat down to dinner, Garrett raised his glass in a toast. "To Laurie," he said.

She cocked her head. "Do you still think of me like that?"

"Sometimes," he admitted. "When I get an idea in my head, I have trouble getting rid of it."

She twisted the stem of her glass, and the wine swirled against the sides. "Once I thought you were in love with Laurie," she said in a low voice.

His face became very still. "What gave you that idea?"

"That would have been a bit too melodramatic, even for this episode," she admitted.

"I suppose so." But he hadn't denied it, had he?

They finished eating in silence, except for the music that surrounded them with its strains of quiet regret. In silence they cleared away the meal. It occurred to her that they worked well together.

The rest of the evening stretched ahead. They would have to retire early to be properly rested for the next day's start.

Janiver offered him coffee and he absently accepted. Then he got out a bottle of brandy, pouring a bit into his cup.

"Want some?" He looked at her questioningly.

She nodded. She sat on the floor in front of the fireplace, absorbed in watching the flames leap and dance. It seemed cruel that anything could look so cheerful when she felt so dismal.

"Tomorrow, with luck, you'll be back in civilization," he commented at last.

She nodded. He leaned against the mantel, cup in one hand.

"Fires always look happy, don't they?" she speculated.

"What?" Hadn't he been listening? He turned to her, a look of near anguish on his face.

Instead of repeating her thought, she simply stared at him. "Garrett?"

He put down the cup with a little bang and quickly knelt beside her.

Their eyes were inches apart. She searched his face, the well-shaped brows, the beard that no longer looked temporary, the dark shining hair waving obediently back from his face. She drew a breath and she felt it catch in her throat. He took her cup from her hand and set it on the coffee table.

"Janiver?"

He closed the few inches separating them, kissed her on the mouth. A light kiss, but it demanded a response. Involuntarily her arms went up around his neck and she clung to him as she returned his kisses, measure for measure. Without thought, without direction, they sank onto the soft Rya rug, lost in the discovery and wonder of each other.

"Stay with me," he muttered between kisses.

After a time he drew back, his finger tracing her lips. "You didn't answer," he said gently.

"Hmm? What?" she murmured, unthinking. She wasn't capable of thought just then, only of feeling.

His hands smoothed her hair and moved downward, stroking gently, pausing briefly where the swelling of her breasts began. Then his lips trailed over her face in light kisses to the pulse in her neck. "I said, stay with me," he repeated softly.

Her eyes flew open. "All winter?"

He nodded, his lips exploring her earlobe.

She lay completely still, no longer responding. He lifted his head to look at her, one eyebrow raised in question.

"All winter," he said definitely.

She seized his hand and turned his palm to her lips, watching him.

His hand against her lips was hard and firm, the hand of an outdoorsman. He took back his hand to frame her face, kissing her lips.

Was he serious? Stay with him? Why? As entertainment against dull winter days?

"Well?" he demanded harshly.

"Why?" she asked.

"Why what?" After a while, his lips continued their distracting course, sending sensations she had never before experienced tingling through her.

"Why do you want me to stay?"

The kisses ceased; he drew away and she shivered.

"Why?" he asked angrily. "Because I love you. Because I want you the way I've never wanted any other woman." Then in sudden anger he sat up, leaning against the brick of the fireplace, running his fingers through his hair.

"Is this too fast for you? I apologize. I suppose I never made it clear that I felt this way, so how could you know? I'm sorry." He was remorseful.

She sat up, too, staring across at him. Between them lay a chill chasm, when a moment ago everything had been warm and close.

"I . . ." she began.

The spell was broken. "I apologize, Janiver. I got carried away. You're a beautiful, delightful woman and I'm . . . ah, human."

"You said . . ."

"Forget it. I'll be all right. You needn't be afraid."

"I know that," she assured him softly.

If he'd been serious wouldn't he have repeated his declaration? Such things were often said in moments of passion, and were not meant to be repeated. Still, she felt bereft, cut off from the warm wonderful feeling they had so briefly shared.

CHAPTER SIX

THEY SAT THERE, acutely aware of each other, denying that awareness.

At last he stood up, then reached down and pulled her to her feet. They looked at each other, and the few inches between them might as well have been an unbridged canyon, a raging wilderness that stretched from her world to his.

Impulsively, standing on tiptoe, she kissed his silky bearded cheek. "For what it's worth, Garrett, you're the sweetest man I've ever met."

For a minute she felt his body tense, then felt the tightness drain from him. He put his arm around her waist and pressed her to his side, companionably, not as a lover.

"Talk about melodrama!" he said, laughing.

He was a puzzle, a puzzle she could not solve right now. She must go away; she must have time to think—time without Garrett.

They made peanut butter and jelly sandwiches and more coffee, and sat by the fire again, talking, talking, talking. They relived the horror of the plane crash and the miracle of the happy ending.

"That was the worst and the best day of my life," he said.

She could not share the memory. She had participated only passively, as the one taken unconscious from the icy wreckage and, unknowing, transported to safety. It felt strange, knowing that a portion of her past would always be lost to her.

Something about the finding of her preyed on his mind, some memory he could not seem to relinquish. She had detected this before and knew her rescue had been difficult for him.

Absently, compulsively, he turned his cup around and around. His other hand stroked her wrist.

"You were so cold," he mused. She nodded. Hypothermia. She knew about hypothermia, as did anyone living in Colorado. She listened quietly, mesmerized by his gentle caress on her wrist, fascinated as he relived that fateful day.

"There was one blanket in the plane, but it seemed pitifully inadequate. I covered you with my jacket, too."

He struggled on, pausing often, always beginning again just as she would decide to prompt him with a question.

"You weren't heavy, though the plane's door was a poorly designed sled and didn't steer well, kept swinging to one side, slowing me down. It took forever to get here, but I suppose it was actually less than an hour."

They had been through all this before.

"You were so cold." He was obsessed with his first impression, his fear that he had been too late.

She turned her hand over, meeting his caress and breaking the trance that held him. He lifted her hand to his cheek.

"I couldn't think of any other way to warm you." It was almost an apology. For what?

She raised her head, wondering what he meant.

"I stripped off your clothes and got you quickly into the bed. Your skin was like ice. I crawled in beside you, hugged you in my arms until finally you were warmer."

This was what he had been wanting to confess. She felt herself blush; she knew she'd have to exercise tremendous self-control or she would blurt out that it sounded very nice, indeed.

"Finally you were warm," he continued, "but it still took another day and a half before you opened your eyes, before I knew you'd live."

Attempting to set a different mood, she said, "I always wake up slowly."

That made him smile. "Just like Sleeping Beauty—waiting for a kiss from her prince.

"You're a romantic, despite your scientific and executive facade," she accused. "And you're not only a rich handsome prince, you're a knight in shining armor, too."

"At least everything ended happily ever after."

"So far."

"Tomorrow will be a piece of cake after what we've been through," he assured her. She believed him, because she trusted him.

The fire had died down into embers and ashes, and he rose to his feet, yawning ostentatiously.

"Bedtime. We'll need every bit of our strength tomorrow."

He said nothing more about her staying all winter. He had just been carried away in a moment of passion. After all, he was a man, a man who had been away from women for some time. Then, too, he liked her; they were friends. And they had shared a close emotional experience that no one else could ever quite understand. She suspected that things would be much simpler for him when she was gone.

"Good night, Garrett." She took her cup to the kitchen.

She puttered around in the bathroom, getting ready for bed, finally crawling under the blankets. But sleep would not come. She tossed and turned, remembering Garrett's admission of how he had brought her back to life and warmth. Knowing they had shared a bed before she had ever seen him, that he had held her in his arms—knowing that somehow changed things.

Everything was so confusing; it would be a relief to go home. What she felt was really homesickness, she decided. She was looking forward to seeing her father again, and Floyd. And Allen, of course.

It was strange, but she could not visualize Allen's face, or capture the feeling of him. Why was that? How absurd of her.

Eyes wide, she stared into the darkness. Her thoughts brought her no repose, and she wondered whether hot chocolate, a traditional remedy for sleeplessness, might help. She eased out of bed and padded to the kitchen, moving as silently as a shadow. No sound came from the couch; apparently the prospect of her departure didn't disturb Garrett's rest in the slightest. Flattering of him to sleep like a log, and after his impassioned plea to stay with him, too!

She turned on the small stove light. The last thing she wanted right now was to talk with Garrett.

The taste of chocolate soothed her. She gazed ahead of her, unseeing, while she tried to marshal her ragged thoughts into tidy legions. The chocolate was finished and she got up to wash the cup.

Garrett stood leaning against the wall by the oven, watching her. She hadn't had the faintest notion he was there. The cup fell from her suddenly nerveless hands, smashing against the tiled floor with a crash, scattering everywhere.

"Garrett! You startled me!"

Without a word he flicked the wall switch, and the room blazed with light.

"What's wrong?" he asked.

"Nothing." Then she added lamely, "I couldn't sleep."

His hair was disheveled from the pillow, but he looked wide-awake, as though he hadn't slept, either. His pajamas of blue thermal fabric were identical to the pair she was wearing. One of his experiments, she thought wryly.

Under his steady gaze, she became aware of her own appearance, hair tangled and hanging limp, no bathrobe, no socks, even. Although they'd been practically living in each other's pockets all this time, she had never felt as vulnerable as she did now.

Her bare feet were in jeopardy from the broken cup, so she stood motionless. Winnie, too, had ambled in to see what they were doing up, and Garrett held her by the collar to keep her from barging through the shards of pottery. "If you'll hand me the broom..." Janiver said formally.

He passed it across to her from the utility closet and she carefully swept the pieces into a neat pile.

Still silent, he handed her the dustpan and she bent to gather up the jagged bits. "Next year test plastic cups," she advised.

That made him smile. "Good idea," he replied.

"Would you like some hot chocolate?" She moved around, collecting milk and cocoa and turning on the burner.

"Please." He shifted a few inches to give her easier access to the stove and cupboard, but he still stood close. She went about her task, heating milk and stirring cocoa meticulously, trying to ignore the obvious tension between them. Finally he moved to the table. She sat down opposite, though she knew she should have left him to his chocolate and returned to her bed.

Irrelevantly she asked, "Won't you be lonely this Christmas?" She could have bitten her tongue as soon as the words were spoken.

"I'm a big boy. I don't believe in Santa Claus anymore." His mouth twisted ever so slightly.

"You won't have any presents or a Christmas tree or..." she said a little sadly.

"There are thousands of Christmas trees outside."

"That's not the same."

"If I wanted the same as every one else, I wouldn't be here."

That was true.

"I still marvel at your being here at just the right time for me."

"Good timing."

She nodded.

After a pause he said, "Mine is the best of all possible worlds." There was an edge of sarcasm, even of bitterness, in his voice. "At least until now it has been," he added in a gentler tone.

"Lucky for me you were here," she said, disregarding the implication. "When you get back to Denver give me a call. If I can help with anything, advertising or whatever, I'll really be glad to do it."

"Really?" He did not seem impressed with her offer.

"To pay for saving my life," she explained.

He studied her a moment, then said, "The Orient has a wise tradition that applies to our situation."

"Oh?"

"When someone saves a life, the one who escapes death becomes responsible for the rescuer's happiness."

That made her responsible for his happiness!

"For how long?" she asked.

"The rest of their lives." He leaned toward her. "Forever."
A little smile hovered around his mouth; his eyes fastened on
her face.

With scarcely a pause she shot back at him, "That's why I
mentioned your Christmas holidays—I'm concerned about
your happiness."

"Of course," he agreed solemnly.

"If I sent you a Christmas card, would it be delivered?" she
asked.

"Eventually." He was looking out the window, away down
the valley, where moonlight on the snow shone almost clear as
day.

"Will you write me, Janiver?" His eyes now rested very
quietly on her face.

"Of course I will. But I want to know that you'll receive my
letters."

"Write on the chance they'll reach me, even if not until
spring." His voice was husky.

"I will," she said, thinking that letters would somehow be
unfulfilling where Garrett was concerned.

She reached for his cup. "I'll call you on the shortwave," she
offered.

"So the whole United States can eavesdrop?"

No, she didn't want that.

Clearly Janiver Parmalee and Garrett Collier were about to
be parted, finally and completely. And it was better this
way, wasn't it? She turned his cup upside down on the drain-
board.

A chill crept through her; her feet were cold. It was the time
of night to be snuggled down in warm blankets.

She scurried toward the bedroom. "Good night," she said,
without looking back at him.

"Good night, Janiver. Sleep well."

As she crawled into bed, the light went out and she heard him
moving to the couch, heard him settling in. She listened, but she
could not tell whether he slept or not. It seemed a long time
before she herself dozed off.

As HE HAD PREDICTED, the sun rose next morning in a clear sky. Janiver woke early, but Garrett was up before her. She lay there, listening to him move around the kitchen. She smelled the coffee brewing, heard the refrigerator door opening and closing. The same as all the other mornings. But today was different. Today she went home. Instead of joy there was a dull ache in her heart, and she felt a numbness she did not recognize.

Guilt at her inaction pushed her from the warm nest of blankets. She would not think about Garrett's having once shared that bed with her, warming her freezing body with his. Perhaps later she could think about it.

As she shoved her toothbrush and comb into her backpack, the curious emptiness inside her grew. Each item stowed in the little bag strengthened the sense of finality. She hadn't expected to feel this way.

"Good morning!"

He was so damned cheerful! He was plainly overjoyed that soon he would be alone again with his thoughts, his dog and his science.

"Good morning, Garrett."

Breakfast consisted of toast, eggs and coffee.

Sunlight streamed through the south windows.

"Nice day," she observed. *God help us,* she thought despairingly. An uneasy silence followed each banal remark.

They were two strangers searching for a common topic of conversation.

Had something vanished with Garrett's impassioned plea for her to stay with him? Whether she and Garrett shared love or simply physical desire for each other, she didn't know. She had wanted him as much as he had wanted her. He was the first man she had ever felt that way about.

Garrett hurried her through the meal, barely pausing for civility, anxious to start the journey. His impersonal air irritated her, but she hid her feelings behind an equally blank mask. He watched critically as she put on her quota of sweaters and topped them with her pink down jacket. The bloodstains had faded innocently, scarcely showing at all.

As they were getting ready to leave, Winnie sat by the door, quietly, soberly, as if she knew that she could not accompany them this time.

"Winnie might bail us out of a tight spot, Garrett," Janiver protested.

"We can't take her. We've discussed that. She'd never make it if we had to climb over a slide."

"But you said . . ."

"I hope it won't come to that, but I won't endanger her life, or ours, by taking her with us."

"Will she be okay?"

"I've taken care of everything," he assured her. "She's been alone before."

"Bye, Winnie," Janiver whispered. "I'll miss you."

Garrett's voice, husky and deeper than usual, cut between them. "Stay Winnie!"

When they stepped into the vast white world, the outside air was as chilly as the atmosphere between them. He was taking pains to avoid physical contact, not to brush her hand when passing her gloves, not to touch her when he fastened her ski bindings.

She seethed. Why was he taking such elaborate care to avoid even the most casual touch? He had lost his credibility as far as she was concerned; his actions made a mockery of all his declarations and pleas.

Finally they were ready. Skis on, packs adjusted, sun goggles in place. The beautiful wintry landscape before them seemed unreal. It had not snowed the previous night and their trail from yesterday led straight to the break in the forest wall. They pushed off, following the familiar track. Behind them, Garrett's house, her refuge for all these weeks, grew smaller and smaller, until it disappeared from sight. The journey had begun.

It started like any of their excursions. Like any of their practice runs. Except that this time, the early morning scene was blurred by the tears in her eyes.

Garrett's appearance suited his role of outdoorsman, with his bright orange ski clothes and a gold woolen cap pulled over his dark hair. His beard and sunglasses effectively disguised his face and hid his thoughts. She saw herself reflected in the dark plastic lenses, but she could see nothing of what he might be thinking.

Her attire was not as professional-looking as his; still, she would stay warm enough. She wore one of his caps, with her blond hair tucked up inside.

"If you've forgotten anything, it's too late now," Garrett commented.

She nodded.

The quiet of the mountainside was deafening. The only sound came from their skis brushing the snow beneath them.

They had started with a rush, as though driven, but Garrett soon slowed their pace. She was glad; her arms and legs were already aching.

"No need to go quite so fast," he cautioned.

It was colder beneath the pine canopy. Each time they passed through open meadow, she welcomed the sun's brief warmth. She wished he would stop in one of the bright warm spots to rest, but he seemed inflexibly homed in on their destination. A few jays fluttered from treetop to treetop, roundly scolding the intruding skiers.

Garrett's citizens band radio was strapped to his waist. Before leaving the cabin, he had tried to make contact with the rescue team, but had encountered only static. When they were nearer, he said, they would be able to talk to the men clearing the pass.

They were more than a mile from the cabin when he stopped to rest in a sunny glade strewn with lichen-covered boulders. The sun's heat was surprisingly intense here. Janiver leaned gratefully against a warm boulder and unzipped her jacket, shrugging it off a moment later and tying the sleeves around her waist.

"Whew!" she gasped. "You travel fast."

Garrett was hardly breathing heavily. He leaned on his ski poles, his face toward her, but his expression was hidden by his beard and the ever present sunglasses. She felt frustrated at not being able to read his mood, and she realized with a pang how familiar his face had become to her over the past weeks. How familiar, and how dear.

A blue-gray bird sat perched on a branch above, observing them curiously.

"I didn't know the jays stayed all winter," she remarked.

"Jays can be anywhere at any time. That's the nature of jays," he said. Then he added with a straight smile, "like me."

They were silent for a time, until finally he announced they should continue. Gathering her strength, she slid her arms into her jacket, pulled on her gloves. Resolutely she pushed off, following him downhill, through more trees.

The day wore on, skiing and resting, skiing and resting. Occasionally they stopped to replenish their strength with chocolate or dried fruit. They seemed to have been traveling forever.

"When will we get there?" she asked.

"Don't worry," he said. "You're doing fine."

Late in the afternoon Garrett again tried the radio, and this time there was an answer.

He gave their location and listened intently as the disembodied voice chattered on at length. It seemed there were problems with the snow removal equipment and the crew would not be able to meet them that night. When the exchange of information was completed, Garrett sat silent and motionless. Then he turned to Janiver.

"We'll have to go back," he said decisively.

"Not on your life! After all that effort!" He couldn't be serious.

His mouth was set in a grim line. "You'll do as I say!"

She swallowed her protest; despite her disappointment, she knew she had to trust his judgment.

"We can rest a while, though." He glanced up at the sun, which now seemed to be edging toward its western resting place.

She got slowly to her feet. "I'm all right. We can start now," she said in a listless voice. Her muscles were beginning to throb with pain, but she was determined not to create a scene.

He didn't move. "No," he said.

"Garrett, you're the most obstinate man," she exclaimed. "You just said—"

"I've changed my mind," he said, his mouth tight.

Tired and exasperated, she wondered what game he was playing now. She'd like to know, so that she could at least learn the rules.

It took all her self-control to keep from screaming at him, to speak in a level tone. "You'll have to explain. I guess I missed something."

He was looking around speculatively, his eyes returning frequently to a spot on the mountainside a little above them where several trees stood near a small creek bed. His gaze followed the slope upward to the top of the mountain.

"Garrett, we're not—" she protested.

"Not what?" But he wasn't listening; he was concentrating on something else entirely.

He pushed forward, propelling himself toward the trees. He couldn't be thinking of camping here, not with night temperatures falling to well below zero.

But it appeared he was considering exactly that.

Her skis reluctantly tracked his.

"Garrett . . ."

"You're too tired to go back. It would take us until midnight, and even then we might get lost. Then, in a day or two, we'd have to do it all over again." He paused. "I can't carry you, not this time." Despite the hint of humor in his voice, she felt she had been a burden to him—in several ways.

"We'll freeze," she said calmly.

"Not if I can help it." He was terse, skimming across the snow between the trees, standing a moment on the rocky creek bank, its water frozen as if in flight.

The site he chose faced away from the setting sun. Darkness and deepening cold swooped down on them.

Three large pines grew beside the silent creek, and two jutting boulders behind the trees gave added protection from a brisk wind.

Garrett fished a knife from his pocket and handed it to her. "Cut as many branches from that tree as you can—about six feet long—" he pointed to a tree that stood apart from the rest

"—and stack them over here." He indicated a spot beneath the tree where they were standing.

Gratefully she shed her skis. Too tired for questions, she did as he'd told her. After several trips, during which she fell and picked herself up more than once, she had built a sizable stack of pine branches. Her gloves were sticky with the resin from the cut wood, but she was too tired to mind; besides, she found the smell rather pleasant.

Garrett was constructing a pyramid of twigs and dry pine needles. With infinite care he placed slightly larger branches around those.

Janiver sagged against a tree trunk, watching. His lighter flared and the flame caught, igniting the little twig tepee, then steadily grew into a respectable campfire. There was no food that needed cooking, so she supposed his fire was meant to boost their spirits. And when it was burning brightly, orange flames pushing back the darkness, she did feel better.

He spit out commands, not requests, as he attempted to speed the camp building. He was a curt, dictatorial stranger. What had become of gentle, considerate Garrett Collier, her rescuer and protector? She didn't much like this man. This man was someone she could leave without regrets.

Warmth stole timidly a few feet from the fire, then dissipated quickly in the cold. It could never keep them alive through the night. In the morning they would be dead, but she was too tired to feel frightened or alarmed, too tired to feel anything. Did it matter whether she died now rather than when the plane had crashed? It would all be the same.

"Janiver!" he barked. "Come here and help me." She dragged her leaden feet over to stand beside him. He showed her how to weave branches together around the base of the tree, how to pile extra snow around the outside, creating a cave of sorts. She obeyed him, trying to imitate his speed and dexterity, twining the branches into as solid a wall as she could. The results looked pitifully inadequate to her. They hadn't a chance of surviving in this cold.

"Hurry!" he urged when weariness thickened her fingers and dimmed her sight. It seemed to take forever, but eventually they had built a little room at the base of the tree.

"I'll never be able to decorate this properly until we get that pole out of the center," she complained from inside, surveying their handiwork on hands and knees.

"Very funny!" he retorted. Pitch-blackness surrounded their tiny island of light. Garrett was still outside, scavenging extra branches, piling them near the fire. He hauled the backpacks over the trampled snow, laying them near the shelter.

He had ordered Janiver to stay inside. The small cave was cramped, but it was better than staying outside. At least here she was protected from the wind, although her feet were chilled almost to numbness.

She glanced at her watch—eight o'clock—hours until sunrise.

Garrett soon crawled in beside her, his bulk silhouetted against the campfire. He was tired, too.

"Why isn't the fire in here?" she inquired.

"Because I prefer to wake up in the morning," he said curtly.

"Oh." Then she remembered her high school science classes and how fire consumed oxygen.

"But if we get too cold, we won't wake up, either," she retorted.

"Our choices are rather limited. We probably won't freeze like this, but we could suffocate if we built the fire inside. There is no perfect arrangement."

"Too true."

He groped through his pack, pulling things out, readying the shelter for the night. One sleeping bag was spread on the snow-packed floor. Then came two lengths of a thin material that shone eerily in the gloom. These he spread on the sleeping bag. The deceptively fragile fabric, she supposed, was another of his experimental products.

"Cold?"

"A tropical island it isn't," she said flippantly, adding in a more subdued voice, "only my feet."

"Get between the blankets."

Her feet were cold and painful. She wished she could shed the heavy boots, but she knew that would be courting frostbite. Lying between the sleeping bags and the sheets of the mysterious shiny fabric, she was decidedly warmer than before.

He slid her backpack under her head. "Pillow?"

After several minutes more of fussing, he crawled toward her. "Move over."

This was no time for self-righteousness, and anyway, it was too cold for mischief.

"Will the fire keep on burning?"

"For a while, but we don't need it now. We've done everything we can." His words had an unpleasant finality.

He rummaged in his pack again. "Ready for dinner?" He produced two foil-wrapped packets and opened two tins of juice.

"Thank you." She maneuvered herself into a sitting position.

"I apologize for not bagging any wild game," he said. "At this altitude there's not much available in wintertime. If we have to stay here several days, I can probably trap a snowshoe hare."

"Garrett, we won't be here that long!"

"This may turn out to be so comfortable we'll want to stay," he said lazily.

"Oh, sure!" She sipped the juice and chewed on the grainy contents of the foil package.

"I really am warm, Garrett," she confided. "There's only one thing..."

"What?"

"My feet are cold. Can I take off my boots? Would I get frostbite and lose my toes?"

"Did you bring extra socks like I told you?"

"Yes, Papa, I did."

"Remember the lesson on feet?" He referred to a conversation they'd had during one of their practice runs. He'd stressed the importance of keeping one's feet healthy when walking or skiing long distances. She had remembered, and now poked through her pack for socks.

It took some awkward wriggling to work off the boots, but finally her feet were free, and she exultantly flexed her toes.

"Stay under the blankets, or you will get frostbite! It works quickly and silently." She snatched her foot back into the warmth of their cocoon.

Thrashing around under the blanket, she pulled clean dry socks over her aching feet. Then came considerably more turning and churning to find a comfortable position. At last she lay still, very conscious of his body only inches from hers.

The cave was actually quite snug, although the packed snow floor felt rather hard and lumpy. But she was tired enough that it didn't matter.

She thought he must be tired, too, even though he was in superb physical condition. He had treated this whole expedition as though it were something he did daily. He lay on his back beside her, his arm almost touching hers.

"Aren't your feet cold, too?" She spoke timidly into the icy silence.

"I'll take my boots off in a minute."

As her muscles began to relax, she discovered just how tired she really was. The day had been long, and they had skied for miles. Her arms and legs ached; the muscles were knotted from exertion.

He raised himself on one elbow to tinker with the radio. At one point they heard an answering voice. Then it was gone and there was only silence.

"We are headed in the right direction, aren't we?" she asked.

"We are. I hope they are. They sounded a bit unsure and not particularly open to suggestions. We're pretty much on our own."

"You mean you're responsible for both of us."

She was enormously conscious of his body lying beside hers.

"What if something happened to me?" he asked into the grayness.

She sat straight up. "Don't say that! I couldn't make it without you."

"Yes, you could," he assured her. But she couldn't; she knew she couldn't. If something happened to Garrett, it would be the end of her. He was either unaware of her total dependence, or he was ignoring her panic.

He awkwardly removed his boots, with the unavoidable turning and twisting. She tried not to notice when his body brushed against hers.

"Are you warm enough?" he asked.

"This isn't nearly as comfortable as your other mountain home," she complained.

A pause. "I asked if you were warm," he said.

She hesitated.

"I take it that means no?" His voice was impersonal, matter-of-fact.

"What can be done? I'm not shivering."

"If you won't think I'm making a pass at you, I'll suggest something."

"Oh?"

"The object is to stay alive. If body heat will accomplish that, it's a resource we should utilize." Good old scientific Garrett! "Unzip your parka," he ordered.

"What?" Her heart thumped in her ears.

His arm reached across her body to tuck the sleeping bag around her. "Unzip," he ordered, his breath warm on her forehead. "We'll huddle together to pool our body heat," he explained.

Slowly she obeyed, and heard him unzipping his jacket, too. The idea made sense, she supposed. He moved closer, turned her to face him until her breasts were pressed against his muscular chest. Warmth flooded through her.

"Put your hands under my arms." His voice was low, emotionless.

Tentatively she slipped her hands inside his jacket, against the rough wool of his sweater. He was warm, and her numb hands immediately felt better. "Your hands are like ice," he accused.

"Are you ticklish?" she asked irrelevantly.

"Don't try to find out," he warned. The idea was appealing and she would have liked to pursue it. Maybe some other time.

Drowsy with the new warmth and her aching exhaustion, she scarcely noticed when he folded his arms around her, cradling her gently, and rested his face against her hair. After a few minutes Janiver slept, warm and safe in Garrett's arms.

She awoke slowly, feeling the silky texture of his beard; her face was tucked beneath his chin. Night had gone, and she could see pine cones through the branches over their heads. Strange that she was warm, with so much snow all around.

She was warm because she was pressed against Garrett. Except for the bumpiness of the floor, she was as comfortable as if she had slept all night in a proper bed.

Sleep fled quickly then, and she remembered that they should have met the rescue team the previous afternoon. She should have been safely off the mountain by now. Allen was probably furious.

Cautiously she stirred, but Garrett's arms held her tight. She peeked at his face through her lashes.

His eyes were shut, his breathing deep and rhythmic. He had worked very hard, she reflected, and he'd been carrying the heavier pack. She lay quietly so she wouldn't disturb his rest.

She closed her eyes, but since she was not sleepy, they soon popped open again. Without thinking, her hand crept up along Garrett's chest, not quite touching him, and stopped at his throat. The tips of her fingers lightly touched the silky hair of his beard.

Suddenly she felt him tense, and realized he was awake. She drew her hand back quickly, but there was really no place to put it that wouldn't be touching him. She refused to look at him, but she knew that he was watching her.

His voice was thick with sleep. "Good morning," he said, then abruptly rolled away from her. She felt like following him, reluctant to lose his delicious warmth. Instead she sat up and looked at him guardedly, almost fearfully.

His clear blue eyes were calm and rested, with no sign of anger. They weren't smoldering with passion, either, and she had to admit she was just a bit disappointed at that. She relaxed, deciding to make light of their intimate sleeping arrangements.

"Success," she said. "It's morning and we're alive."

His lips twitched. "Success. I held you in my arms all night long," he said softly.

She felt herself blush and, to cover her confusion, reached quickly for her boots, ignoring his words.

"How cold do you think it is this morning?"

"Can't tell. I'm quite comfortable myself," he drawled, enjoying her embarrassment.

The cold tempted her to dive beneath the blankets and return to his warmth. Instead she concentrated on lacing her boots, and carefully smoothed the tops of her wool socks.

Her feet were still sore in places, but she was beginning the day almost as good as new. Thanks to Garrett. Thanks to his knowledge of survival. Thanks to the warmth of his body—again.

Garrett. Tomorrow he wouldn't be beside her. She stopped dead, her fingers poised unmoving over one unlaced boot.

"Hungry?" His voice came from directly behind her, businesslike and courteous. There was no hint that anything more intimate than a casual greeting had ever passed between them.

"Yes," she whispered. "I'm starving."

Without warning, she was pulled back into the warm nest of blankets. She lay looking up at Garrett face above hers. Too startled to struggle, she stared as his mouth descended toward hers. She closed her eyes, not thinking, savoring the feelings he aroused in her. Her arms found their way around his neck and she arched against him, giving herself up to the demands of his strength.

The sound he made as his lips moved lightly across her throat was almost a groan, almost a sigh of contentment. His lips nestled beneath her earlobe, and she thought he murmured, "Laurie." Then she felt him draw away. She lay still, her eyes closed, expecting him to pull her close again. But there was only the chill morning air, tempered by the protective shelter they had built together the night before.

Slowly she opened her eyes. He was sitting up, hiding his face in his hands.

"Garrett," she said softly, not moving.

"I'm not sorry," he said belligerently.

She gathered the sleeping bag around her shoulders, huddling there in a misery that had nothing to do with the bleakness of their makeshift shelter.

He suddenly grabbed his boots, then crawled to the entrance. She opened her mouth to call him back, but no sound came.

After a time she rummaged for packets of rations and fruit juice and dragged herself to the door of the shelter.

Garrett was standing just outside. Without speaking, he moved to make room for her. Quickly she zipped her jacket and pulled down her cap—no point in losing the night's comfort.

They faced the sun, which hovered a few degrees above the horizon; it was early yet. Below them the white slope stretched forever, sometimes interrupted by stands of pine and outcroppings of red boulders. The air was so still she could hear the silence. This beautiful place had existed, virtually unchanged, for centuries. Its serenity was completely untouched by her disquiet, and she found that fact strangely comforting.

Within twenty minutes they were on their way. The clear morning air brought good radio communication with the rescue crew, who were, indeed, headed in the right direction. They expected to meet Garrett and Janiver only a few hours later.

She could almost believe that his kisses inside the shelter had never happened. But she knew they had.

As they headed for the trail they had broken the night before, she glanced over her shoulder. The remains of their pine branch and snow shelter was now indistinguishable from its surroundings, and only the blackened campfire showed that anyone had recently been there. The trampled area would be covered over by the next light snowfall or by the drifting wind.

No one would ever know that Garrett Collier and Janiver Parmalee had been there. They could have slept their final sleep in that place and no one would have known until spring.

She dared not look directly at him; he would know her thoughts if he saw her face.

She followed him down the slope, skiing easily, settling quickly into the routine. She concentrated on matching Garrett's pace, though he skied like a demon, striding over the snow, determined to attain his objective.

For two hours they skied and rested, watching for signs that they were not alone on Shadow Mountain. Before noon, when they paused once more, Garrett cocked his head, listening.

"Can't be sure we're hearing the source or the echo," he commented. Janiver nodded.

The mountains stretching away on all sides seemed to go on forever. Maybe they would never find the rescue team.

Then, from far off, came the drone of motors. Garrett pointed to a vee between two mountains. "There they are!" he exclaimed. And in the distance they could see what looked like a procession of tiny black ants, crawling steadily toward them.

CHAPTER SEVEN

AS THEY CONTINUED the ants had become a convoy of high-way equipment methodically attacking the mountain of snow. The plows chugged along, clearing the asphalt roadway, exposing it inch by inch. Behind them crept a caravan of toy cars and trucks. They stopped when they reached the slide area.

"No sign of the helicopter," Janiver commented from where they stood.

"No landing pad," he said shortly.

Radio communication was excellent now, and they chatted sporadically with the rescue team.

How could they best traverse the slide area? Should they wait where they were and let the snowplow risk being swept away in coming to them? Or should the plow stop and wait for them to come over? Being lighter and faster, they seemed to have the better chance.

To the background sputter of the plow, Garrett and the crew leader debated the pros and cons of various plans.

Finally the decision was made. Janiver and Garrett would take the last mile, and they would do it as quickly as possible, since the sun was already casting long shadows.

They faced the gigantic white-gray mound of ice chunks mixed with soft snow, uprooted pines and displaced boulders, all flung down casually by an avalanche. To their left yawned a gorge, its steep sides pocked by rocks and twisted trees.

"This is the best way?" Janiver asked incredulously.

"Hard to believe, isn't it?" He smiled grimly.

She nodded, speechless. How could they possibly cross this...this valley of death? Garrett helped her remove her skis, inspected her boots and asked anxiously if her feet still hurt.

She shook her head, not altogether truthfully. He tied one end of the rope around her waist, fastening the other end to his own belt.

"I'll go first," he said.

"Can't we go together?"

"No."

Her hands were sweaty inside the gloves, and there was an empty feeling in the pit of her stomach as she prepared to follow him. The path, if it could be called so, was narrow and clung precariously to a rocky ledge.

"Ready?" he asked.

His voice sounded so forbidding that she merely nodded. He looked at her a long moment and she thought he was about to say something. But then he turned toward the obstruction that had kept her a prisoner on Shadow Mountain.

"Let's go," he said.

She held her breath when he stepped onto the ledge. They had no way of knowing what lay ahead, but they were depending on that ledge. They fervently hoped it extended all the way around the slide and would in time bring them to the highway. He inched several tortuous yards away from her, at each step probing the snow with his pole, testing the footing. When the rope between them had lost almost all its slack, he beckoned her to follow him. Concentrating on Garrett, forcing herself to ignore the steep drop, she inhaled deeply and stepped onto the ledge. Her hand grasped the branch of a tree for support.

Her progress was painfully slow. Each step had to be tentatively explored. Then she had to shift her weight to the front foot. And then came the process of lifting her other foot and setting it down again. Garrett waited until she was within arm's length.

Foot by foot, yard by yard, the two figures crept across the face of the jumbled white slope. The rescue team stood by, nervously waiting and watching.

Janiver saw only Garrett. Her eyes were glued to him as her steps followed his. Her muscles were strung so tautly she felt they would surely snap. Her eyes burned from not blinking.

It seemed hours later when she became aware of voices, words of encouragement cheering them on. Still she saw only Garrett, calmly, doggedly, going forward, inch by inch, step by step.

Now they were only a few feet from the voices. Rough hands reached out to pull them over a railing. Unbelievably they stood on solid ground—an ordinary blacktop road. A confusion of faces swam before them. Smiling, congratulatory strangers who thumped them on the back and mouthed incomprehensible words. Janiver blinked, slumping in exhaustion. After the silence of the past weeks and the tension of the past hours, the din was almost overwhelming.

A battery of cameras with long lenses stared at them like so many eyes; the sound of film was like the buzz of rattlesnakes on a hot Colorado day.

And there was Allen, pulling her into his arms, looking closely at her face, then smothering her in a clumsy hug.

And there was Art Herbert with a gold 15 pinned to the collar of his ski jacket.

"Welcome back, Miss Parmalee. I'm Art Herbert!" He shook her hand enthusiastically.

Relief at having crossed the gorge successfully and pride at accomplishing what they'd set out to do became all mixed up with exhaustion.

Janiver swayed. Allen caught at her shoulders, his hands colliding with Garrett's, who had reached for her from the opposite side. The trio stood frozen for a moment before she recovered. "Excuse me," she gasped. "Allen, this is Garrett Collier. Allen Tobin."

The men acknowledged each other coldly.

"I'm all right, really." She shook free of them both.

Dusk was already descending, gloomily creeping through the trees. It was cold. They would have to start down soon.

Allen took her arm. "Ready, Jan?" he asked.

She glanced around for Garrett, then saw him talking with the crew leader. She moved toward him. Instinctively he seemed to know she wanted to speak to him, and interrupted his conversation to turn to her.

She held out her hand formally. "Thank you, Garrett."

He closed the space between them, clasped her hand in both of his. "Goodbye, Laurie." He spoke in a low voice. She wished he would take off the damned sunglasses—she wanted to see all of his face.

There was still so much to say. They had not, after all, said everything. They must do something about this attraction that sparked between them. But not now.

"Are you coming to Monarch, Garrett?" she asked, assuming that he would be getting into the car with them.

He shook his head, gesturing toward a man in a parka. "Bill has a house a few miles from here. He's an old friend, and he's also the area ranger. In fact, he's been helping the rescue crew since yesterday afternoon. Bill and I will have a chance to catch up on things tonight. I'll head back tomorrow. I can't leave Winnie alone for much longer." Her hand still lay in his, warm and safe. Of course he had to get back to his experiments—and to Winnie.

"Well—" she scarcely felt Allen's tug at her arm "—have a Merry Christmas."

Garrett's smile broadened. "You, too. And a Happy New Year!"

Then Allen pulled her away.

Her legs threatened to collapse completely and she climbed awkwardly into the waiting four-wheel-drive vehicle, grateful to sit down at last. Allen got in beside her, expansive and jovial, crowding the back seat.

Janiver turned for a last look out the rear window, but they were already rounding the curve and she could no longer see Garrett. Still, she stayed turned, watching the receding view, acutely aware that she would not see him again for a long time.

Suddenly she realized that someone had asked her a question and was waiting for an answer. "I'm sorry." She shook her head groggily and straightened herself to look at the others in the car. "What did you say?"

Art Herbert's eyes had already recorded her physical condition, and she braced herself to hear the next day's newscasts describe her as tired and dazed. Though that was accurate enough.

"May I call you 'Janiver'?" His smile flashed like an advertising sign. She nodded weakly. Allen regarded Art Herbert with a half smile on his lips, patent admiration in his eyes.

"Are you well enough to tell us about the plane crash?"

The rich voice was polite though determined. Janiver knew that her chances of resting were slim until she had recounted at least the outline of her adventure.

For the past two days, every ounce of her energy had been directed toward getting back, to covering the miles of rock and snow separating her from home. Now she would have to put everything into some kind of perspective. But it was difficult even to remember that day when she had taken off from the prairie landing strip. Allen patted her shoulder, his arm wrapped around her.

For a full minute she sat quietly, watching the snow-dusted mountainside gliding past outside. Then she began at the beginning and went straight through, covering the highlights of what had happened.

Monarch's first streetlights slid past the car windows as she described camping out the previous night, virtually the end of her story. "Garrett thought it would be better if we stayed there, since we were so close and we hadn't been able to meet you," she explained. She felt Allen's arm tighten around her shoulders.

Herbert nodded, his face bland. "And how did you keep from freezing to death? The thermometer went well below zero."

She told how they had built the fire and how they'd used branches and piled-up snow to make the shelter at the base of the tree. A look of respect dawned on Art Herbert's face. "Well!" he said. "I give Mr. Garrett Collier full credit."

"I owe him my life," she said simply.

"Yes, I understand that, don't you, Allen?" But Allen was staring out the window, his mouth tight, a muscle in his jaw clenching and unclenching.

They stopped at a rustic but quaint hotel with a coyly primitive sign advertising rooms and a restaurant.

After they had run the gantlet in the lobby and closed the door of the suite, Allen generously assigned her the bathroom and one of the bedrooms.

"Your father sent along some clothes," he informed her.

"My father—where is he? There was so much commotion I—I assumed he'd be meeting us here."

"We'll see him in Denver tomorrow," Allen said.

"He isn't sick, is he?" she asked anxiously.

"No, no, not at all. Apparently there was an emergency at the ranch—I don't know all the details. I only found out at the last minute that he wouldn't be here."

After a warm bath and a session with makeup and a hair dryer, Janiver put on tan corduroy trousers and a navy sweater. What a joy to be warm and clean again! Allen had insisted on having dinner with her in the suite, though she would have preferred some time alone. She needed time to reflect, to absorb the experience on Shadow Mountain. Time by herself.

As they had arranged, she joined Allen for dinner—complete with a bottle of champagne.

Promptly an hour after they had left him in the lobby, Art Herbert turned up. He made himself comfortable on the couch while Janiver devoured her dinner. The prime rib was perfect, considerably more appetizing than the dried fruit and rations she and Garrett had subsisted on for the past two days.

Herbert coughed discreetly, brandishing the microphone of a small tape recorder. "Janiver, any comments on how if feels to be stranded for over a month with one of the most eligible men in the world?"

She paused. "Who? Garrett?" She supposed the question shouldn't have surprised her after her father's hints, but it still came as a shock. She couldn't quite grasp what these cheap insinuations had to do with her. Or with Garrett.

Allen shrugged and gave her a patronizing smile. "Darling, you must know about Garrett Collier."

Of course she knew about Garrett Collier; she knew a great deal about Garrett. She knew he was a dedicated scientist, and yet a thoroughly practical man. She knew he had a sense of humor, knew he was intelligent and resourceful and courageous, knew... yes, she knew many things about Garrett Collier.

"Such as?" she hedged, clutching her glass and nervously swallowing champagne.

They watched her like two vultures waiting for a stumble.

"She doesn't read the gossip columns," Allen apologized for her.

Art Herbert was quick to enlighten her with a capsule commentary on the status of Garrett Collier.

"He just happens to be one of the richest men in America, and most single women would give anything to be stranded with him in an isolated cabin on top of Shadow Mountain."

Janiver raised her eyebrows. "Really?" She hadn't suspected that Garrett enjoyed such a reputation. It meant she and Garrett came under the heading of Romantic Interlude. Interesting. And she suspected that Art Herbert knew exactly what he was doing. He was getting more than a wilderness survival story; he was getting an opportunity to make the episode sound like the romance of the year, which of course it wasn't.

"So I would like your reactions," Herbert persisted.

She dug her spoon into the chocolate mousse.

"Garrett Collier saved my life. He and his marvelous dog dug me out of a plane wreck and kept me from dying. I was halfway to either heaven or the other place when he rescued me." The words came out quickly, smoothly, matter-of-factly.

Herbert gave her a long speculative look, then clicked off his tape recorder. "I can see you're tired, Janiver."

No, she wasn't tired, not anymore. She was wide-awake now and ready for any traps he might try to set for her.

"He's right, Jan," Allen interposed. "Enough is enough. You need rest."

She rose and went to the window that looked down on Main Street. "Monarch is coming into its own, isn't it?" she commented neutrally.

"One of these days Monarch will be another Aspen, only better," Allen answered. She remembered he'd invested in a real-estate venture here.

Minutes later Art Herbert took his leave; his farewells were polite but rather curt. Probably because he hadn't been able to pry any morsels of gossip out of her or trick her into any incriminating statements, Janiver thought furiously. She closed the door sharply behind him. "What an odious man!" she stormed.

Allen still sat at the table, his half-empty champagne glass loosely held in his hand.

"Jan," he began.

She turned her back to him, looking out the window at the mountain, a dark, dim mass rising behind the town. One of those winking, mocking lights up there marked the house where Garrett was that night. She should have insisted he come to Monarch with them. He should have been answering some of Art Herbert's questions. He shouldn't be getting off scot-free in this search for a sensational news story. There wasn't one; it was that simple. So why should she have to cope with the interrogations all by herself? Garrett should be here, too, talking with Art Herbert—and with Allen.

No. That would have complicated things unnecessarily. That wouldn't have been fair. Besides, it was her fault the world was looking at them; she should be the one to suffer the consequences. Had she not been so heedless of danger in the first place, this whole thing would never have happened.

She realized Allen was talking, that he was waiting for an answer.

"I'm sorry, Allen, what did you say?"

A look of irritation crossed his face, and he lifted his champagne glass and drank a long draft.

"You'll get better headlines if you're a little more cooperative with Art," he advised sullenly.

"Am I not being polite enough to that creep?"

"No," he replied, although his lips twisted at her epithet.

"He's evil," she said flatly.

"That's ridiculous, Jan, and anyway, it's beside the point. He engineered this rescue. His station put up thousands of dollars to be in on the great moment."

That was none of her doing, none of her concern. Her father could easily have handled the whole thing, but Art Herbert had taken over. And Allen, for reasons of his own, had thrown in his lot with Art Herbert.

"So I should give him a good show for the money, right?"

"I didn't say that exactly."

"Do they want all the lurid details?"

He leaned forward. "Are there lurid details?"

"Of course not," she snapped, turning once more to the window and the lights up on the mountain.

After a while Allen phoned for the table to be removed, though he kept back the unfinished bottle of champagne.

If he had any amorous ideas, she was going to squash them. She was very tired. Allen had changed—or was she the one who was different now? She no longer seemed to be the same person, the Janiver Parmalee who had set off in November for a ski weekend in Steamboat Springs.

She closed the draperies, shutting out Monarch's picturesque Victorian streetlamps and the troubling lights on the mountainside. Of course, none of the lights could actually have been Garrett's cabin; that was her imagination.

"I'm very tired, Allen," she said in a prim voice.

"But we haven't finished the champagne." He tried to sound jovial but didn't quite succeed.

She walked to the door of her bedroom and turned toward him, yawning widely. "Thanks for everything, Allen," she said politely. "Good night."

She shut the door and, after a slight hesitation, locked it. Then she threw herself on the bed and buried her head in the pillow.

On Allen's side of the door, something hit the floor with a thump.

Damn Garrett! Why wasn't he here to see her through this mess? The feeling of wanting to get away from him had vanished, gone with their last touch, that impersonal handshake on the mountain.

"Damn, damn, damn!" She pounded the pillow in frustration.

After a long time, she dragged herself up from the bed and stumbled into the bathroom. It wasn't possible that she was homesick for Shadow Mountain. No, it wasn't possible at all.

AROUND MIDMORNING THE NEXT DAY, they left Monarch under gray skies. A light snow paved the roadway before them. Could Garrett get back to the cabin in this kind of weather? Who would feed Winnie if he didn't?

There were cameramen in the dining room, the lobby, the parking lot, all storing up scenes and images to be edited later for the ten o'clock news.

The car turned onto Interstate 70, slashing its way through the falling snow. Eyes closed, head against the window, Janiver was soon sound asleep. When she awoke, they were emerging from the mountains above Golden, the metropolitan area stretching miles before them to the east. Disoriented, she sat up sleepily. Herbert explained they would go directly to the TV studio, so she combed her hair and freshened her makeup.

Their arrival at the studio was recorded by still more cameramen. And at last there was her father.

"Dad!" She flew to him, throwing her arms around his neck.

"Everything's all right, baby!" Tears ran down his tanned cheeks, and she patted his shoulder comfortingly.

"You scared me to death, you little brat!" he scolded, holding her away from him and shaking her gently.

"I scared myself," she admitted. "You wouldn't believe how quickly that storm came up. And the forecast—"

"You know you can't depend on those dudes," he growled.

Allen interjected at this point, snaring her with a possessive arm. "Well, she's home now, Mr. Parmalee." He wanted his share of credit.

The older man's eyes narrowed. "Thanks to Garrett Collier, I understand."

"That's so," Allen conceded stiffly.

"I want to meet that man, Janiver," her father informed her.

"Garrett? You want to meet Garrett?"

He nodded. "I have a great deal to thank him for." It occurred to her at that moment that Garrett and her father would get along famously.

When they returned to the ranch, Floyd shed unashamed tears. "You know, Janiver," he confessed, "I've been feeling bad about that little disagreement we had before you took off that day."

"Oh, Floyd, I'm sorry, too! You were absolutely right, I shouldn't have gone. If I'd listened to you, I'd have stayed out of trouble."

He beamed. *But if I'd listened to Floyd,* she thought, *I'd never have met Garrett.... Anyway, I'm home!*

She was home! The first day she slept until noon. The second day she called the modeling agency. The third day she paced the house like a caged tiger.

The weeks with Garrett were a tear in the fabric of her life, a tear that she somehow had to patch before she could carry on.

Denver glittered with Christmas decorations. Stores and shops and TV programs were all tinsel and wreaths and blaring carols. She found herself viewing these things in a new light; what had once seemed festive now struck her as tawdry and commercial. This Christmas there was more comfort for her in the stark purity of the new-fallen snow than in the strings of colored lights and cleverly decorated trees.

She watched newscasts featuring her as the lead story. She looked remarkably fit, considering how close she had come to death. Newsmagazines included a few paragraphs about the rescue in their People sections. All the hype would be over within a month.

The publicity surrounding her escapade had made her more in demand than ever. Less than a week after her return, she discovered that ad managers were eager to use the beautiful face that had recently appeared in the news in the company of Garrett Collier, millionaire adventurer. She had thought him simply a scientist enjoying a private winter. Feeling a mixture of chagrin and guilt, she thought once again about how her intrusion must have complicated his life.

Her agency had scheduled her for a swimsuit layout in the Caribbean. She would leave Denver the second of January. That gave her time to celebrate, though she felt anything but merry. Christmas without the weeks of preparation was scant fun. She remembered Garrett's teasing words, asking her whether she wanted a doll for Christmas. The memory was bittersweet.

Garrett...

He was constantly in her thoughts. Art Herbert had called a few days earlier to say that Garrett was safely back at the cabin on Shadow Mountain. She had reacted politely, noncommittally. But after hanging up the phone, she had sagged thankfully against the wall. Garrett was safe.

The initial excitement of being home again, of seeing her father and Floyd, had worn off. Somehow now she felt... incomplete. She told herself that once she readjusted to her real life, the empty feeling inside her would go away. She would remember Garrett Collier as the man who had rescued her, nothing more.

Allen invited himself for Christmas dinner since Janiver had refused his repeated pleas to spend the day with him. If she couldn't be with Garrett, then she belonged here, with her father.

Floyd boosted the Christmas spirit by single-handedly decorating the house and shopping for their dinner, hauling in an enormous turkey, with cranberry sauce and as many other trimmings as he could find in the supermarket.

"Floyd, do you realize this bird is the ghost of leftovers yet to come?" Janiver teased, although she was grateful to him for taking over and injecting some enthusiasm into the season.

He looked sheepish. "Won't we need this much?"

She patted his arm. "I'll put some in the freezer and you and Dad won't need to cook while I'm sunning in the Caribbean."

He brightened. "It's all right, then?"

"Of course. Thank you, Floyd. You're making Christmas Christmas." At least he was trying; it was her own fault she didn't feel merry.

"You haven't been the same since you came back, Janiver," Floyd said.

She busied herself putting away groceries. "I'm getting back into the swing of things."

He shook his head. "No, that's not it." His leathery face was earnest.

"What do you mean?" she asked cautiously.

"Well, Jan, you aren't telling us everything that happened up here, are you?"

"Floyd," she scolded. "Now you're acting like a reporter."

"No." His innocence was obvious. "But . . . what's Garrett Collier really like?" he asked after a slight pause.

She carefully stacked tins on the pantry shelf. "He's very nice," she hedged.

"How nice?" he persisted. Floyd had gone straight to the very heart of the matter. Just how nice was Garrett?

"I'm trying to decide that myself," Janiver said honestly. But she couldn't look at Floyd. He let the matter drop then, pressing no further. For the moment.

Christmas dinner would be the four of them: her father, Floyd, Allen and herself.

In the frantic, busy pre-Christmas days, she had made time in between last-minute modeling assignments to shop for Allen's present. Wandering through the shopping mall, she was suddenly aware that she really didn't know what he might want for Christmas. She had barely any idea of his special interests or his tastes.

In contrast, she saw countless items that would have been perfect for Garrett. At nearly every shop there was something else that would amuse him or intrigue him. But she didn't need a gift for Garrett Collier.

Allen arrived late Christmas Eve, and Janiver felt obliged to make some kind of effort at hospitality. She threw together a slapdash supper and poured them both a glass of wine.

When Allen had finished eating the meal she'd served him, he sat at the table, watching her clear away the dishes. She was acutely conscious of his eyes on her.

"Jan?"

"Yes?" She looked up from rinsing off his plate.

"Jan." He cleared his throat nervously. Then he was standing beside her, a small package in his hand. Her heart sank. The time had come to exchange gifts. Couldn't they have waited until the next morning?

"I want you to have this now, while we're alone."

The beautifully wrapped package lay like a burning coal on her palm. "Allen," she began.

"You shouldn't have—" he finished with a show of humor.

"You really shouldn't," she insisted.

"I wanted to," he said softly.

There was nothing to do except loosen the ribbon and begin tearing away the paper. The box's shape suggested either a bracelet or a wristwatch. No doubt it was something for her antique jewelry collection. Everyone knew she loved art nouveau.

Everyone, apparently, except Allen. Inside the expensive wrapping, inside the box, lay an ultramodern gold watch. She smothered her disappointment and turned a polite face to him.

"How thoughtful, Allen. It's beautiful!" But her enthusiasm was pure pretense.

He claimed a kiss, but she kept it short and friendly. She freed herself, holding him off with one hand. "Now it's your turn!" she called as she escaped to fetch her gift for him.

If he was disappointed in the impersonal sweater, he hid it well, though she watched closely to see if he was as let down as she had been.

Christmas day went no better. Despite red poinsettias all around, the atmosphere was leaden with her father's lack of congeniality; attempted conversations consistently sputtered and died. She felt only relief when their turkey dinner was over and Allen drove away.

Her heart and mind were elsewhere. What was Garret doing? How had he celebrated this Christmas day?

She could not explain her preoccupation with Garrett Collier. She had wanted so desperately to get back to her own life. Had he meant it when he'd asked her to stay with him? The bittersweet memory of that moment haunted her. She still remembered, still relived the safe secure feeling of sleeping in his arms...the thrill of his touch. She must put him out of her thoughts once and for all!

DRIVING TO DENVER TWO DAYS LATER, she parked outside the modeling agency and hurried into the building. The bright sun belied the winter season and ridiculed the garlands and wreaths still hanging in the lobby. Leftovers, like the turkey sandwiches and casseroles Floyd and her father would be eating for days and days.

She entered the chic, carpeted office and greeted the receptionist. There were still some arrangements to be made for her Caribbean assignment, though she already knew who her photographer would be—John Clifford. That was a break. He was very good; in fact, he'd done the Laurel ad.

One of the secretaries handed her a packet containing airline tickets and other essentials, all the while looking at her as though she were a celebrity. Janiver's life would never be the same again.

When she returned through the outer office, she almost collided with Art Herbert. "Good morning, Janiver!" The smooth familiar voice sounded unsurprised.

She frowned slightly. Why was he here? Surely her story was old news by now. "Good morning, Mr. Herbert."

"Call me 'Art,' please!"

The words tumbled out before she thought. "What are you doing here?"

"Picking up background." His smile was overfriendly.

"Oh? Doing a story on the modeling profession?"

"In a way."

"Not about me, I hope."

His speculative look swept impersonally over her. "You're an interesting subject."

"Why me?"

"Why not you?" His voice was impatient, almost accusing. "You're beautiful, and not only that, you're a successful model. You pilot your own plane. People are intrigued by that. You crashed in the mountains—and lived. You possess special qualities—courage and the survivor instinct. You're a logical subject for a feature."

She had no reply.

"Will you join me for coffee?" he asked.

She couldn't think of a valid reason to refuse. He held the door open for her, then followed her through.

After a mild discussion in which he tried to persuade her into his car, they arranged to meet at the Brown Palace twenty minutes later.

The nineteenth-century lobby of the vintage hotel was still a gathering place for Denver's rich and famous. Art Herbert and Janiver crossed the white marble-floored room. As they headed into the dimly lighted coffee shop, he placed his hand on her elbow, steering her to a secluded table.

A waitress brought two cups of coffee, and Janiver wrapped her hands gratefully around the cup, drawing heat into her chilled fingers. Art Herbert sat silently, as though pondering how to begin the conversation. Finally he asked, "Have you adjusted to civilization yet?"

She had been surveying the room, idly looking at the other customers. At his question, she turned reluctantly toward him. "Yes," she said, smiling sweetly. "I think so."

"Christmas?"

"Was very nice," she lied.

"And Tobin—Allen?"

"Is fine, thank you." What did he want from her?

"Have you heard from Collier?"

That must be it. "No. Have you?" she said politely.

"Did you see our news items on your rescue?" He had obviously decided to try another approach.

"Yes. Did it increase your ratings?"

His smile grew into a grin. "Now, now, Janiver, do I detect a note of sarcasm?"

Her blue-gray eyes widened in surprise. "What?"

He suddenly leaned across the table, and the scent of his after-shave was strong and too sweet.

"You don't like me, do you, Janiver?"

"Does that bother you, Mr. Herbert?" she said, not denying his assertion.

He watched her for a moment without answering, his eyes narrowed. "No, it doesn't bother me at all." After further pause, he asked in a deceptively casual voice, "Are you in love with Garrett Collier?"

She jumped, startled, coffee sloshing over the sides of her cup. "What gave you that idea?" When she looked at his face, she knew he was satisfied with her reaction.

"Just a hunch."

"Who wants to know?" She hoped she didn't sound too defensive.

"Everyone wants to know if the beautiful girl-pilot is in love with the rich, handsome bachelor who rescued her—and if he's in love with her. We might have the romance of the year right in our backyard."

"It's nobody's business!" She shouldn't have said that. She should just have laughed the whole thing off.

His face had taken on a sly and hungry look, and his eyes gleamed with the thrill of the hunt. She tightened her grip on the coffee cup to keep from hurling it at him.

"Is it possible to be that close to such a charismatic man without feeling some physical attraction for him?" His tone was confiding—and insulting.

"Of course it's possible. Don't forget, I was injured." Unconsciously her hand went to her temple, where the scar was hidden beneath a wave of thick blond hair.

"So you say."

"I have no intention of showing my scars to the American public," she said angrily. Then, before he had a chance to continue his insinuations, Janiver seized the offensive. "What do you have against Garrett?" she asked, wondering if he would give her an honest answer, if he would admit why he wished Garrett ill.

It was his turn to look surprised, though he quickly assumed a bland expression. "We go back quite a few years," he said evasively. He paused. "Look, I'll tell you the truth. I'll do almost anything to get a good story. I can't put it much plainer than that. Garrett Collier makes for a good story. You and Collier are an even better one."

"What's so blasted special about Garrett Collier, anyway?" she burst out.

"He's merely one of the richest men in America, Janiver." Art drawled each word with exaggerated patience, as though incredulous that she still didn't understand.

"I don't happen to keep little black books with the bank accounts of America's single men," Janiver retorted scornfully. "It's nothing to me if he's rich or poor. Your insinuations are completely wrong. Garrett's personal life is his business—not mine."

She took a deep trembling breath, pushed her cup aside and stood up. Glancing down at Art Herbert, she shrugged into her coat, a look of distaste on her face. Still holding her breath, she walked quickly out of the coffee shop, uncomfortably aware of his eyes boring into her back. She crossed the foyer's white marble floor and stepped out into the winter sunshine. Only then did she release her breath.

Janiver worried about the incident the length of her drive home. She had insisted so adamantly that Garrett's personal life was none of her concern, but she knew this wasn't the truth. Why else was she constantly thinking about him, constantly speculating about his relationships with other women? He'd never mentioned having any special woman in his life. There had been no personal pictures. Of course, she hadn't seen into every drawer, but drawers were not where men kept pictures of women they loved.

But Garrett's love life was no concern of Janiver's, was it? Perhaps if she kept reminding herself of this, she might actually come to believe it.

THREE DAYS LATER Janiver flew out of Stapleton Airport aboard a commercial airliner, headed for the Caribbean and her swimsuit assignment.

She welcomed the new surroundings and the demanding schedule, hoping time would solve her unsettled state of mind. The daily photograph sessions on the white sandy beach became a spectator sport for island natives and tourists alike. Although the swimsuits were relatively modest, she felt very much on display. A colorful tent had been set up as a dressing room. A crowd of small dusky children would ooh in rapture as each model emerged from behind the tent flap to walk barefoot to the cameras.

Between poses, Janiver would stroll along the beach, where the turquoise sea reflected the cloudless sky and powdery sand squished between her toes. She would wade in the water's fringe, fascinated at the white ruffles endlessly capturing and releasing her steps. But her thoughts always returned to Shadow Mountain. Garrett would have been intrigued by the contrast between this sandy beach and the deep snow that lay outside his cabin, she thought.

So many things reminded her of Garrett. Her feelings about him tumbled riotously around, floating out of reach whenever she tried to catch them and pin them down. She made an effort to discipline her mind and tried to substitute Allen's face for Garrett's. Without success.

One afternoon when she returned to the dressing tent, a grubby little boy with snapping black eyes ran up to her and thrust out a handful of postcards.

"You buy, *señorita*?" he inquired hopefully.

Janiver shook her head, indicating she carried no money.

He grinned, understanding perfectly, and pointed inside the dressing tent as he pushed the cards into her hand.

"Money, *señorita*?"

"All right, you little supersalesman, wait here. How much?"

He understood that, held up ten fingers. She chose three traditional beach scenes intended to strike envy in the heart of anyone left behind in snow country.

"Gracias, señorita!" The dark-haired elf swept her a courtly bow, pocketed the coins and darted down the beach.

Janiver smiled after him. Garrett would have cared about the boy's future, too. But Allen, she reflected, would have been more concerned with the cheapness of the purchase. That evening she would write them both, and her father.

Inside the dressing tent she picked up her next costume change—a black bikini well suited to her blond hair and golden skin. The bruises from the plane crash were almost gone. One scar on her shoulder still remained. She covered it with foundation makeup, then slung a colorful towel across that shoulder.

Did Garrett ever think of her? What was he doing now? Skiing the rounds of his sites, no doubt, and keeping his carefully accurate logbooks. And when work was done, what would he do? Would he sit down to study? Would he stare out the window at the snow and the trees? Or would he write a letter— a love letter to someone she had never heard of?

CHAPTER EIGHT

JOHN CLIFFORD, THE PHOTOGRAPHER, had invited all three models to dinner.

The hotel capitalized on its tropical-island setting by arranging wrought-iron chairs and tables among palms and rubber trees in open courtyards.

Janiver's blond hair made her highly visible and the object of a great deal of attention. She was wearing her long hair coiled smoothly around her head, and her dark cotton dress was fastened at the shoulders by thin rainbow-colored straps. The dress nipped in at the waist, accentuating its tinyness, then flared to below her knees. Her shoes were a frivolous concoction of straps that tied around her slender ankles.

Mariachi music thrummed through the crowded room. John Clifford and Sheila, the brunette, were engaged in a semiserious flirtation, leaving Janiver and Cassie either to converse with each other or seek greener pastures.

Cassie's hair was a beautiful titian. The three women were a study in contrasts; each had been chosen to fit a particular stereotype—blonde, brunette and redhead. Every man in the restaurant feasted his eyes on the striking American girls.

Janiver reached into her purse, taking out a pen and the postcards. "Excuse me, Cassie. It's not that I'm tired of your company—I just want to send these cards."

Cassie tossed her shining coppery head. "No problem." Her brown eyes searched adjacent tables for someone interesting, pausing here and there before moving on.

Janiver wrote first to her father, then dashed off the message to Allen. She picked up the card intended for Garrett and wrote the address, then stopped. What would she say? Something funny? Something trite?

Something only the two of them would understand, whatever that might be. The pen was poised above the blank white space a long time.

"Dear Garrett..." No, not *dear*; it sounded too...something.

She chewed the pen. "Hi!" That was better; it was casual, noncommittal. "Here I am—" she nearly scratched that out, then changed her mind and continued "—stranded on a tropical isle."

Comical and trite had won. She finished the message with a neutral remark that told him nothing of what she had been feeling since the last time she'd seen him. She remembered every second of their parting. His hand holding hers. The frustration of not seeing his eyes, of only seeing herself reflected in his sunglasses. Even with all the photographers and reporters, she should at least have kissed his cheek. But that might have given her away. A simple kiss was not always simple.

After dinner, she paused at the front desk to buy stamps and mail the cards. Almost as soon as Garrett's card had slipped through the slot, she regretted the inane message she'd written him. She could still get the card back and throw it away. She started to signal the desk clerk to retrieve the card.

"Excuse me." The voice was strongly accented, and she turned to look into the face of a handsome dark-haired man she had never seen before.

"Yes?"

He bowed. "You are very beautiful."

She drew back, ready to retreat.

"Do not go," he said. "I wish to talk with you." She'd heard that line before!

"I'm in a hurry." She drummed her fingers on the desk.

He went on. "I think you are one of the American models shooting pictures for a magazine.... Swimsuits?" That information was not exactly confidential, however, and she still viewed him with suspicion.

Janiver prepared to slip past him and run for the elevator. Cassie had disappeared into the bar. No help there.

"I very much apologize for not waiting for an introduction, but you see there is no one here whom I know, and so it would be impossible." He shrugged, and an appealing smile flashed across his thin face.

Janiver sidled closer to the elevator.

"My name is Jean DuChamps." He waited for a reaction.

"Oh?" she said politely.

"In Paris, my models are very much in demand."

Oh, that DuChamps! The House of DuChamps represented some of the most beautiful women in the world. Was he telling the truth?

He drew a business card from his pocket and held it out to her. The card confirmed his words. But why was he talking to her?

She smiled tentatively. "I'm sorry. I didn't realize who you were, though of course I've seen your pictures countless times."

His smile broadened. "And I yours. I have, in fact, instructed my people in the States to contact you. I believe you have recently completed an adventure." Even he had heard.

"The whole world knows about my adventure," she said tightly.

"I have wondered how my friend Garrett Collier is."

He was a friend of Garrett's! She had to know more about that. She allowed herself to be led into the cocktail lounge, allowed him to order two glasses of champagne and orange juice.

When the waiter had gone, she turned eagerly to Jean DuChamps, asking him, "How do you know Garrett?"

He studied her animated face a moment, his handsome Gallic features hiding his thoughts. "I know him very well," he answered. Had he deliberately misunderstood?

Her eyes still questioned him, and he continued, "Although our businesses are of a different nature, we meet socially and share common interests." Did he mean Garrett shared Jean's interest in beautiful women? Somehow Janiver didn't think so.

As they talked further, it became clear that Jean DuChamps did indeed know Garrett well. He described how, one summer, they had both participated in the Red Zinger bicycle race in Colorado.

Jean's talk of the bicycle race set Janiver thinking, visualizing Garrett clad in tight black shorts and striped shirt, his powerful legs pumping. She could imagine the look of fierce concentration on his face. She knew he would compete vigorously, with wholehearted enjoyment. That was the way he did things.

Garrett. She had a sudden painfully clear memory of him, a memory so intense it was almost physical.

"You do not look at all like the survivor of an airplane crash," Jean broke into her thoughts. "You have no scars, I think."

"None that can't be concealed," she said with a laugh. "I was fortunate."

"I begin to think Garrett was the lucky one," he said, his Gallic charm very evident. Compliments from this charming Frenchman were nice, but a little discomfiting to someone from the laconic American West.

They chatted easily for another half-hour, until Janiver discovered with a surprised glance at her watch that it was already ten o'clock.

"I really must go, Mr. DuChamps. Tomorrow we start shooting early in the morning."

He nodded. "I shall speak with you again."

He escorted her to the elevator, and when she extended her hand to bid him good-night, he kissed it in the continental fashion. "Sleep well, Mademoiselle Parmalee." She retreated into the glass-fronted elevator, watching him as she was wafted upward to her floor. Jean DuChamps was unsettling and utterly fascinating.

As she entered the dining room the next evening, Jean DuChamps stood and bowed, inviting her to dine at his table. John Clifford looked surprised, and whistled under his breath. "Don't turn down the House of DuChamps," he advised. "We'll see you later, Janiver."

Cassie gave her a little shove in Jean's direction and Janiver stood alone, feeling abandoned. She hesitated a moment, but only a moment, because Jean shepherded her to his table and seated her across from him.

When they had sat down, he leaned forward, smiling. "Ah, Janiver Parmalee, and how are you this evening?" His lilting pronunciation of her name delighted her. "I trust your working day went well?"

"Yes, very well," she replied.

"I confess I joined the crowd of spectators to watch the shooting session. I noticed that you work very hard—much harder, for instance, than the one with the copper-colored hair."

She didn't know quite what to say to that, so she settled instead for studying the menu. Was DuChamps so attentive because he was Garrett's friend, or did he intend to ask Janiver to join the House of DuChamps, as John Clifford seemed to think?

Dinner was superb. She didn't have to agonize over her selection, because Jean suggested the conch and she agreed, certain that his taste would be impeccable. This man's business was beautiful women, after all, and he knew how to charm.

"Have you flown since the accident?" he asked halfway through dinner.

She hesitated. "Not my own plane. I suppose I'm a little frightened of going up again."

"It would be most unusual and unnatural if that were not the case," he assured her.

"When I get home, I'll take my courage in hand."

"It is important that one get back on the horse again after falling off, no?"

She nodded agreement. Garrett had said much the same thing.

After dinner, they went for a leisurely stroll along the beach. A three-quarter moon stood just above the horizon, its reflection a silvery path across the water. Quiet waves lapped endlessly at the sand.

When they had turned back and nearly reached the hotel again, he stopped.

"Janiver . . . Miss Parmalee."

"Yes?"

"Do you know about the House of DuChamps?"

"Of course!" she said.

"I mean, do you know how we do business?"

"I understand it's not like other modeling agencies." Her heart skipped a beat.

"We are quite different, quite unique."

Incredibly he seemed almost to be offering Janiver a position. She waited silently for him to proceed, unsure of what to expect.

"If you like, I will explain the differences."

"Why?"

"Ah, Janiver Parmalee, one of your greatest charms is your direct American approach." She heard the smile in his voice. "I am inviting you to enter the House of DuChamps," he continued, his voice as formal as his phrasing.

Surely she hadn't heard correctly!

"Then I would very much like an explanation of the differences," she said as calmly as possible, though she thought he must hear her heartbeat above the sound of the sea.

"Come, let us discuss this." He led her to an iron bench on a small terrace and gently urged her to sit. He explained how the models who worked for the House of DuChamps were offered only choice assignments, were always treated with consideration. Then he went on about fees and contracts. He gave her time to absorb all this before he continued. "I have already told you of asking my American representative to contact you. Sometime ago several photos of you were brought to my attention."

Janiver shivered in the warm humid air. She felt as though the whole world were watching her, from the sleaziest tabloids to the elegant House of DuChamps. She couldn't help resenting her loss of privacy, though she knew she should feel honored by Jean DuChamps's offer. And she did. It was something no woman in her right mind would refuse.

"I..." she began.

"Perhaps you need time?" The smooth gentle voice conveyed genuine understanding.

She stood up on shaky legs. She wanted to run, to hide where no one could ever find her or ask her to make such a monumental decision.

"Yes, Jean, yes," she said breathlessly. "I must think. I—it's—you're very kind."

"You will wish to discuss the idea with your family and with your agency, who would, of course, receive a substantial fee in lieu of your future services. Perhaps you will wish also to discuss it with Garrett Collier," he suggested.

"Yes," she gasped. "Good night!" She fled across the tiled terrace and into the bright foyer and up the stairs, too impatient to wait for the elevator. She leaned against the inside of her door, breathing hard—almost as though she had just escaped some danger. After a few minutes, she was able to stagger across the room, stripping off her jewelry and shoes as she went.

The House of DuChamps! Paris! London! Rome! The best designers! She looked at herself in the mirror. Except that her eyes were wide with shock, she looked the same as she had when she'd dressed for dinner.

She didn't feel the same.

She threw herself on the bed and picked up the telephone, dialing her father's number. She heard the series of clicks that signaled the connections being made across the miles, until finally, she heard his deep comforting voice.

"Hello."

"Dad?"

"Jan? Anything wrong?"

"No," she said. "No. I just wondered how things were at home."

"Nothing special. The weather's been lousy the past few days. How's the sunny Caribbean?"

"Marvelous." But she didn't sound convincing, even to herself. He was probing, trying to find out the reason for her call. She knew he still felt anxious about her.

"Not good flying weather?" she asked.

"No, not at all."

"Have you talked with the insurance people about my new plane?" He would think that was why she'd called.

"They're getting the paperwork straightened out. Probably be ready when you get back."

When she got back. "Great! I think it's time I went up again."

There was a pause at the other end. "Oh, by the way, Jan."

"Yes?"

"You've got a letter here."

"Who from?"

"No return, but it was mailed in Monarch, Colorado."

Monarch. Then it must be from Garrett, mustn't it? That meant he had written to her even before she'd sent him the postcard.

Why was her heart beating so fast, when the letter might only be an advertisement from the Timber Hotel? But she could not wait to get home and open the letter. She managed to say, calmly enough, "Just put it on my desk, Dad."

"That's what I did, honey. We'll be seeing you."

"Bye."

Slowly she hung up the phone, reluctant to break the link. All thoughts of Paris and the House of DuChamps had vanished because of one unopened letter from Monarch.

Later, of course, she realized she could not close the door to DuChamps, after all. Jean had told her to think the offer over carefully. She would.

The morning they left for Miami, Janiver spoke with him briefly. "I will see you in a short time, I think, Janiver Parmalee." His eyes, more than his words, warned that he would not be put off with an indeterminate answer. He pressed his business card into her hand. "Do not lose this," he cautioned. Janiver's smile felt frozen on her lips.

Then they were off, going home. At last. They changed planes at the busy Miami airport, and the sun was drifting behind the Rockies when the huge plane eased into a landing at Denver's Stapleton International Airport.

Floyd and her father were waiting for her when she arrived. She embraced them and followed them out to the car, huddling inside her coat. After a week in the sun, she wasn't quite prepared for winter. Once they were back home, there was much to be said about the trip and about the ranch before she could finally escape to her bedroom. She sped across the carpeted floor to search her desk.

The letter lay in the center of the bare desk top. As she reached for it, she remembered what she had written to him. Carefully she slit the envelope with her fingernail and unfolded the single sheet of white paper inside. "Dear Janiver..." He hadn't ducked the traditional salutation, as she had, she thought.

But the actual message was awkward and stilted, not the sort of letter she would have expected Garrett to write.

"Winnie goes all over the house, looking for someone." He hadn't said the dog was looking for her.

"Have a good Christmas." Her eyes darted to the date at the top of the page. This had been written only days after their parting. He had missed her! She felt giddy with the joy of it.

"By the way, you forgot your nail polish." So that's where it was!

She read the letter again, and her mood sank. On second reading, the words seemed merely flat. But there was still the fact that he had written her so soon. He had been lonely. Or was it merely polite concern? *So much for your precious isolation and its interesting effects,* she thought.

There was no reason to read the note over and over again; the words remained the same, though her emotions shifted with each reading. Resolutely she folded the paper and slid it back into the envelope.

"Jan?" Her father knocked lightly on the door.

"Hi, Dad!" Briskly she lifted her suitcase onto the bed and opened it.

He crossed the room to sit down in the armchair near the desk. Although he did not appear curious, he must have noticed the opened envelope.

"The insurance company came through—just this morning," he said. The significance of his quiet statement took a moment to register.

"Oh, Dad, that's great!" She ran to kiss him on the cheek. "When do I get the new plane?"

"If you can find a copilot and some time off, you can fly it back from Wichita anytime."

"Oh!" Was she ready? "But *Little Susy* wasn't new. I thought the insurance company would replace her with a plane of equal value."

"Guess they wanted to be specially nice to you."

She eyed him with suspicion. "Did you go extra for a new one?"

He looked sheepish. "Well . . ."

She threw her arms around his neck. "You doll! Thank you!"

Now she had to fly again. There would be no backing out after her father's generous gesture.

THE NEXT DAY, as she sat down to toast, coffee and orange juice, Janiver picked up the morning paper. Skimming the first page, she saw a small photograph of herself in one of the little squares that promoted the day's features and urged readers to look inside. She turned to page twelve as directed.

There were, in fact, two pictures. One was of her shaking hands with Garrett in that last moment on the mountain. The other showed her in a brief black bikini she'd modeled just a few days earlier. Unknown to her, at least one of the crowd of "spectators" had been an opportunist. *They missed getting me with Jean DuChamps,* she thought cynically, *or will that come later?* She scornfully dismissed the picture.

But the shot of her and Garrett on the mountain she studied intently. Was there any hint in either face that might suggest there was something intimate between them? Nothing that she could see.

A few trite phrases accompanied the photos. Journalism of this kind never bothered with full explanations or worried much about the accuracy of its information. Janiver had become the property of that segment of the press that spoke in captions and headlines, insinuating much but saying little.

She returned to the picture taken on the mountain. Garrett stood in his heavy clothing and backpack. She remembered her almost shy thanks to him. She had thought that surely they would see each other once more before he started back. But Allen had prevented that.

Allen. At least now she was sure of her feelings about him. The romance was dead—if, indeed, it had ever been alive. She wondered how it could have taken her so long to become aware of his insensitivity, his boorish possessiveness. She couldn't even remember why she had been so anxious to get to Steamboat Springs to see him.

Carefully she tore out the newspaper pictures. She'd think about them later. Right now she had more pressing things on her mind, because she and Floyd were flying to Wichita the next day to bring back her new plane.

When she dropped in at the office that afternoon, she was told the agency head had asked to see her. She climbed the curving staircase of the renovated mansion and tapped on the door of Mike Kearney's private office. She waited for his summons before she entered. As always, she was impressed by his tasteful office, with its windows fronting on the Rockies and its elegant antique furniture.

"Sit down, Jan."

Mike Kearney was not only businesslike, he was popular with his staff and his clients. His warm personality and his sincere concern made him easy to talk to, and Janiver had never hesitated to approach him with problems and questions. Now he leaned back in his chair and regarded her with a faint smile. "Had a good time down south, I hear," he said. The remark was meant to bait her, in a friendly way.

"Suppose you tell me what you've heard," she said with a smile.

"Fame is making you cagey. No longer the honest true blue Colorado beauty who shoots from the hip," he teased her. Then his manner changed and the laughter fled from his voice. "Seriously, I've had half a dozen phone calls from a certain gentleman in Paris."

"Oh, that," Janiver said.

"*That* is the opportunity of a lifetime, Ms Parmalee," he said solemnly.

"I haven't decided what to do. I wanted to talk with you." Her lowered eyelids hid her feelings.

"Most women would have jumped on the plane with Du-Champs and dared me to come and get them."

"I'm sure you know I'm not 'most women,' Mike."

"When will you decide?"

"I'm off to Wichita tomorrow to pick up my new airplane."

He raised his eyebrows. "Hmm. Doesn't sound like you plan to move to France. I thought you might hold off on flying for a while, after what happened."

"I've held off too long already. I have to get back in the cockpit and I should have done it before now, but things kept getting in my way."

"Like several feet of snow on the ground?"

"And Christmas, and notoriety, and swimsuits."

"Sorry about that last one."

"It's all right." Her words were light as dandelion fluff. "What would it mean for you if I did go with DuChamps?" she asked, trying to keep her voice casual.

"It would mean we'd lose a valuable property," he admitted. "But DuChamps is eminently fair, and he'd make it worth our while. Having you go with them would lend prestige, and it would give us first chance at the best-looking girls in the western United States."

"All that?" Now she'd have to take the agency's welfare into account when she made her decision.

He nodded solemnly. "All that."

She raised her eyes and saw a news clipping on his desk. It was the same one she had torn out that morning. "I see you're monitoring my press coverage," she commented.

"When I can. The notoriety will probably last a few months. Then it will die down and things will be back to normal. Nothing you can't handle. That is, if you manage to stay out of the spotlight in the future." He spoke with finality, as though there could be nothing left to say on the subject. Then he leaned forward in his chair and said conversationally, "So you're off to Wichita?"

"Yes."

He stood up and extended his hand to her across the desk. "Good luck, Jan. Check in when you get back."

Descending the gracefully curving staircase, she realized she would have to decide about DuChamps, and soon. Opportunity knocked only once.

Home again, she found a phone message from Allen and irritably pushed it aside. She didn't feel like talking to him right now; she'd call him when she'd returned from Wichita.

She sighed as she thought about all the decisions waiting to be made, all the questions waiting to be answered. But first she would get her new plane and see if she could fly it as though nothing had happened, as though her life had not completely changed course.

THE NEXT MORNING Janiver and Floyd were on a commercial airliner, headed east toward Kansas. Beneath them rippled a brown landscape of dry creek beds and rolling hills gradually flattening into prairie.

It was noon before their cab turned into the gates of the aircraft factory. The next hours were spent inspecting the graceful blue-and-white beauty that was her new plane as Floyd fired questions a mile a minute.

Floyd's inquisition dragged on. The company representative looked exhausted, though Floyd was still tinkering, still inquiring and still accepting answers skeptically.

Over coffee and apple pie, Floyd drilled her again and again on the differences between the new plane and the old one. She rubbed her sweaty palms on her jeans as she ran through the familiar motions of piloting a plane. Then it was time.

She sat gingerly in the cockpit, felt the wheel, fingered the controls. "What if I can't do it," she gasped.

"Why wouldn't you be able to?" Floyd growled.

Janiver took a deep breath, then began to feel more comfortable in the craft. Grateful for Floyd's quiet presence, she manipulated the controls and slid the plane down the modest runway. She lifted its nose and they were off, heading west, a wind blowing southwest to northeast against them.

They glided across Kansas, and then Kansas became Colorado. They could only tell where the boundary was by reading the navigation charts. It all looked the same from above: the same prairie, the same rectangular fields, the same barbed wire fences.

Presently the Rockies unfolded on the horizon. They seemed modest enough at first, becoming more and more imposing as one realized that beyond the first range of peaks there were others stretching on for hundreds of miles. At Stapleton, the little plane set them down as gently as a mother would a baby in a cradle. Next to her, Floyd released a long-held breath.

"You needn't hold your breath about my flying, Floyd Nolan!" she scolded. He muttered something unintelligible, but she was paying no attention. Her only thought was that she had done it. She had flown again!

CHAPTER NINE

BRIGHT SUNSHINE SMILED on blue mountains and brown plowed fields as Janiver drove into Denver on her way to a photo assignment. Despite the chill in the air, she and another model were scheduled for a spring-fashion layout against some of the city's landmarks. That meant working quickly to take advantage of the shreds of midday sunshine. It also meant that backgrounds had to be carefully chosen to disguise the fact that spring had not yet reached Denver. But that was not Janiver's job. Her job was to pose where she was told. Yet there were things she would rather do today than shiver in shorts and halter top. Things such as playing in the snow with Winnie, or talking with Garrett.

Usually she could push Garrett from her mind, but other times, like now, he was there so clearly that she almost expected to look over her shoulder and see him.

It happened whenever she saw a golden playful dog like Winnie. It happened whenever she saw a brown-haired bearded man in the distance.

The plane crash, the time with Garrett, the trek back and the accompanying notoriety—it was as though they all had happened to someone else, not Janiver Parmalee. Not to her.

She reached the photographer's studio and parked her car in a reserved space. She ran up the low wide steps to the studio, carrying her makeup kit and an extra sweater.

She heard someone call out, "Happy Valentine's Day, Janiver!" as she entered the building.

She had forgotten this was Valentine's Day. She should have sent a card to Garrett. But she had been caught up with flying again, with proving she could pick herself up after a fall. Valid as those excuses were, she suspected there was another reason. Had she managed to forget the date because she hesitated to commit herself on the day set aside for lovers? She and Garrett were not lovers, though the thought sent chills up her spine. She shook her head and concentrated on listening to the photographer's instructions.

The day passed quickly as Janiver and the other model, Christy, obediently stood, sat and reclined in preselected spots, wearing preselected outfits. Janiver tried to capture the mood of each costume, blending mood with background. Modeling was basically a selling job. And the fact that DuChamps wanted her meant she was good at what she did. She would have to decide—soon—about the House of DuChamps.

Back at the studio, she dashed in to return the costumes, then pulled on her own jeans and snuggled into the heavy brown sweater.

The car's heater warmed her. Maybe she would stop to buy a valentine, after all. She turned into a small shopping square that included a card shop.

Tomorrow all the red-hearted, lace-trimmed merchandise would be obsolete for another year, but now there was still a varied selection. Janiver examined the obligatory heart-shaped cards. Too sweet and sentimental, she decided. The humorous ones seemed impersonal, and the cards that were meant to be loving and tender struck her as insincere.

She stopped. Was it facetious to be looking for the perfect couplet to send to Garrett? Wasn't it juvenile? When the idea had first occurred to her, she had thought it amusing. Even charming. But now she felt it was merely childish and inappropriate—he'd think it was silly.

She turned abruptly and left the shop, almost stumbling through the door onto the sidewalk.

"Jan!"

She looked up, scarcely registering. "Oh. Hello, Allen."

He took her arm. "I tried to call you last night," he said.

She had been home all evening, so he couldn't have tried very hard. Not that it mattered. She smiled politely.

His voice lowered intimately. "I wanted to spend Valentine's Day with you."

She stared at him blankly, and had to stop herself from asking why. She supposed this was as good a time as any to end the relationship, such as it was. The irony of breaking up with him on Valentine's Day did not escape her. Halfheartedly she agreed to dinner at a small French café on Capitol Hill.

After Christmas she had known for sure there was nothing real between them. Whatever attraction might once have existed had long since died. She sighed wearily. It was only fair to clarify the situation, she supposed. She would tell him before dinner. And if he changed his mind about having dinner with her, she'd understand. In fact, she didn't think she'd mind at all.

Their table was small and fairly secluded, set at an angle to the rest of the room. They had just ordered their wine; Allen was perusing the menu and Janiver was screwing up her courage to broach the unpleasant subject.

"Good evening, friends!" The familiar voice invaded their privacy without permission.

Allen stood up and heartily shook Art Herbert's hand. 'Well, hello! How are you?" Janiver aimed a polite smile in the direction of the smooth bland face.

Why was Art Herbert still "accidentally" showing up in her life? It wasn't as though they had established a friendship. Quite the opposite. Each time they met, she was left seething with anger and suspicion. There was no "story" in Janiver Parmalee's life, except for the one coincidence that had caused her path to cross Garrett Collier's.

But Art Herbert was interested in Garrett, not in Janiver Parmalee.

She had a sudden feeling of dread. Had something happened to Garrett? Was that why Art Herbert had come here like a vulture circling to feed off her unhappiness?

She stared at one man, then the other. No, Art and Allen were too low-key for anything so dramatic. She breathed a relieved sigh. If anything were to happen to Garrett, she knew she would not be able to hide her feelings.

She sipped Chablis, her eyes downcast, as she let their meaningless conversation flow around her.

Then abruptly Art Herbert got up and bade them goodnight.

Janiver watched the tweed-coated figure wind his way between tables, push open the leaded-glass door and disappear into the night. She was tempted to ask what Art's appearance had all been about, but decided the topic was best left alone; there were more pressing things on her mind than Art Herbert's opportunism.

"Allen," she began. She might as well get it over.

"Yes?"

"I've got something to say and I should say it before you treat me to dinner."

"That sounds ominous. Is everything all right?"

"Oh, yes. I'm fine," she said.

There was nothing to do except to tell him straight out, make things as plain as she could. "Allen, after tonight I don't plan to see you again. I'm not the least bit in love with you, and it's not fair to pretend that I am." There, she had said it, and he couldn't possibly misunderstand.

He took the ultimatum calmly. "I understand." He paused. "There's someone else?"

"No." She moved the silverware around as though the table were improperly set, which it wasn't.

"I hope we'll still be friends," he said.

"That's all it can be, Allen, friendship." She wasn't apologizing and he knew it. He raised his glass to her, his eyes blank, no warmth, no hurt. Nothing. "To your future happiness, Jan, whoever you choose to share it with."

She touched her glass to his. "Thank you," she said in a steady voice. Then, to the waiter's relief, they ordered dinner at last.

Conversation limped along, stiff and polite, and they plodded civilly through to the end of the meal. But despite the awkwardness of the evening, Janiver felt as though a burden had been lifted from her.

At her car she held out her hand in final farewell. "Thanks, Allen. For everything."

He retained her hand for a moment. Then he pulled her gently to him and kissed her forehead. "I wish you'd never met him," he said with a hint of bitterness.

She knew who he meant. "No, Allen, you're wrong," she protested.

"So you say." He opened her car door. "Goodbye, Janiver Jarmalee."

She drove away with a little wave of her hand and left him standing in the dark parking lot, the streetlight behind him, hiding his face.

She was finally starting to take charge of her emotions. Allen was out of her life. No more trying to convince herself that he really wasn't such a bad sort. No more guilt about unmet expectations, no more halfhearted feelings of obligation. She was free!

Ever the gentleman, Allen had summed it up gallantly. "To your future happiness, whoever you choose to share it with."

Were her feelings for Garrett that obvious? "I wish you hadn't met him," Allen had said. Where had all the suspicions begun? Not with Garrett's chaste goodbye on the mountain. Not with anything she had said. Had something shown on her face? Any tenderness, any closeness was locked deep within memory—hers and Garrett's.

When she reached home, she went straight to her bedroom and pulled out the letter, the one proof that he had not dismissed her from his mind the minute she had rounded the curve in the road.

She threw herself into the upholstered chair by the window, where she could see all down the Platte Valley, could see the lights winking against the velvet-dark setting. There was no moon tonight, so she could not see the mountains a few miles away. If she drove two hundred miles west on the sleek four lane highway slashed through rock and forest, she would be almost at Garrett's doorstep. If those highways had never been built she would still be there—stranded in Garrett's cabin.

The lights along the valley mocked the confusion of her thoughts. She groaned and hit her clenched fist against the arm of the chair. "Damn! Damn! Damn!"

The letter lay crumpled in her lap. Hurriedly she straightened it. She read it once more. There was no explaining her feelings. She had shown Allen the door. She was lonely. She was dying for the sight of Garrett Collier.

Did he look the same, she wondered. Suddenly she had forgotten how he did look! There was no image in her mind, only a name—Garrett Collier—and a feeling. A feeling she could not define.

She got up, paced the rose-colored carpet between the neatly made bed and the full-length pier-glass mirror in the corner of the room. After several rounds she sheared off in the direction of the bathroom.

She pulled her sweater over her head, discarding it on the floor.

Garrett, Garrett, Garrett.

Suddenly she saw him clearly in her mind, felt his arms holding her. The image struck her so sharply, so intensely, that she stopped in midstride.

My God, I am in love with him! It was that simple. She was in love with him. All her confused emotions, all her scattered thoughts made sense now. *Love.* She had finally put a name to the unfamiliar feelings, and everything seemed to fall into place. Slowly she unbuttoned her shirt.

Janiver reached for the towel, closed the bathroom door and turned on the shower. She shivered as the spray hit her body. What if Garrett loved someone else? She didn't think she'd be able to stand it.

The pelting drops smoothed away the long day's aches, melting the tension that had gripped her since her confrontation with Allen.

She stepped out of the shower, wrapped the towel around herself, crossed to the desk and picked up the letter reading it for the thousandth time.

Suddenly she remembered his words—*"Stay with me."* He had wanted *her*, Janiver Parmalee. She remembered the night in the shelter on the mountain, the feel of his body as they lay together, warming each other, keeping each other alive.

She would write him. By now he must have received her insipid postcard, although it was possible the card still lay in a postman's pouch or in a cubbyhole at Monarch's quaint little post office.

She tapped her bare foot impatiently on the soft carpet. The weather was fairly good now. February was half over; winter was winding down. If she were to drive to Monarch she could cross Shadow Mountain Pass and ski to Garrett's place.

Whether he wanted her or not.

Could she get there without anyone knowing? She would not want the world to witness her rejection. She would not want Art Herbert or any photographers to be there when she saw Garrett again.

The idea gathered momentum, growing like a snowball in her mind. Once in Monarch, once on Shadow Mountain, could she find her way to Garrett's cabin? She would have to get there by herself, show up at his door without warning.

She would know when she saw his face how he felt about her. She would know, and if there was any doubt in his face, she would leave at once. The idea was insane. She would do it. As soon as she got a map of Shadow Mountain, as soon as her work schedule permitted, as soon as she could arrange to borrow her father's little pickup truck, she'd leave.

The preconditions she set up, the obstacles she built in her mind—they were excuses, weren't they? Because she was afraid, because she could not really imagine how it would be, seeing Garrett again. What would she say? What would he say?

She pulled her nightgown on over her head and stood one last minute with the lights off, gazing out the window toward the mountains. But they were hidden from her by the darkness.

Of course, she could just wait until he returned to Denver. That would be in a month or two. All that time in which to wonder and fret—it would feel like an eternity.

She fell into bed at last, and exhaustion silenced the argument.

TWO WEEKS LATER she drove west on Interstate 70, past Denver's skyscrapers, through the notch in the foothills that took her across the hogback, into the Rocky Mountains.

Anyone watching the ranch gates early that morning would have seen a young person of indistinguishable sex, clad in denim jacket, jeans and a cowboy hat, drive a blue pickup truck through the gate and turn onto the highway. An observer might have guessed the driver to be a young ranch hand off for a load of hay, judging by the empty back of the pickup.

It was drizzling when she left. She could see puffy clouds tucked here and there in the foothills, and knew that higher up, the rain would change to wet snow.

The trip stretched ahead, hours alone on the road. Time enough to think about her insane mission. Time enough to turn back. No one except her father knew she was doing this, so no one would witness her loss of nerve. And her father had been reluctant to see her undertake this trip at all; he'd simply be relieved if she'd cancel it.

She drove on. All morning, storm clouds played peekaboo with the sun. The rain washed the boulders so that they glistened when the sun briefly shone. Water escaping from the melting drifts streamed over rocks and fallen trees to dash through culverts beneath the roadway.

After a quick lunch and a walk to stretch her legs, she climbed into the truck again, ready to continue the journey. She tossed the wide-brimmed hat into the passenger seat, her blond hair spilling luxuriously across her shoulders.

By midafternoon the intermittent showers had turned to wet snow, and she drove more slowly, windshield wipers working diligently to reveal the pavement before her.

The likelihood of reaching her goal faded when she rounded a wide curve and found a line of traffic stopped dead on the road. She braked, halting a few feet behind a yellow school bus full of teenagers.

Patience wore thin and gas tanks emptied as the long line of automobiles waited. And waited. And waited.

Janiver tapped her fingers impatiently on the steering wheel. Her plan was falling apart. Was this a sign that she should forget the whole thing, turn back before she made a fool of herself?

It seemed that a mud and rock slide had blocked the way, and road crews were slow in clearing the debris. And even if it was cleared, it wasn't certain that all the traffic could get through. Nor could anyone say how soon the road would be passable.

Some cars had already turned back, and Janiver was in a quandary. With her finger marking where she was now stalled, she studied the map, searching for a likely place to stay the night. Monarch itself looked no more than twenty-five miles away, though much good that did her. There was, however, an alternate route, winding off to the right, a lower quality, longer road.

Not completely sure of her next move, she, too, turned around and headed back the way she had come. She would decide whether to take the turnoff shown on the map when she got there.

The road would eventually lead to Monarch, but first it passed through a place called Glory Hole, which she had never heard of. Venturing down the road would be taking a chance. The wisest move would be to go back to Vail, where at least there were accommodations.

Janiver put aside the map. She decided she would go to Glory Hole. Soon her pickup turned onto a narrow asphalt road threading into a heavy growth of trees. She drove slowly. Darkness was now complete, and her headlights pushed it forward a few feet at a time. Now and then wisps of fog drifted eerily in front of her. It seemed as though she had been driving forever; her legs were cramped and she was tired of sitting. Several miles back the gas gauge needle had settled on Empty, but the engine still ran, dutifully and purposefully. Soon she came out of the trees and saw a welcome sprinkle of lights ahead. She had arrived at Glory Hole.

But Glory Hole wasn't much. She prayed there would be a place to buy gas.

A dimly lighted service station stood by the road, and she thankfully pulled up beside the lone gas pump.

"Thank goodness you're open!" she exclaimed. "I'm nearly out of gas."

"Came in on hope, eh?"

"Definitely!"

The attendant grinned as though the joke would have been on her had it not been for Glory Hole's gas pump.

"Is there someplace near here to stay the night?" she asked. "Motel?"

"Or a hotel. Someplace clean."

"New place up the road a couple miles," he offered, sauntering back to unlatch the hose from the pump.

As she followed the man's simple directions, she passed the remnants of Glory Hole. It had once been a gold mining town, but was now little more than a straggle of houses clinging to a few unpaved streets.

Glory Hole Lodge was set back from the road on a half-circle drive. A modern rustic sign proclaimed the name and the amenities: restaurant, rooms, heated pool. It sounded perfect. Half an hour later, she was ensconced in one of the last available single rooms. She obviously wasn't the only stranded motorist to take advantage of the lodge; the place was buzzing.

This journey she had undertaken in a fit of insanity wasn't going well. She should have stayed home. If Garrett wanted to see her he knew where she lived. He could have written another letter.

She dug into her purse for the one letter she had received from him, opened the worn envelope and took out the single sheet of paper, though the bland, conventional words were etched deep in her memory.

She would not go on to Monarch tomorrow. She would go home.

She laid the letter on the dressing table and flung herself across the bed, burying her face in her hands. She was tired; it had been a long day. She fell into a short fitful sleep.

When she awoke it was dark and silent. There she was, alone in a strange room, and somehow that made her feel even more foolish at coming this far. She hoped she would not run into anyone who recognized her.

She was ravenous. She would have to get up and dress, then go and look for the dining room.

A fire-colored blouse with a soft ruffle at the high neckline set off her hair and skin. She pulled her blond hair into a chignon—practical, but elegant in the way it accentuated her high cheekbones.

Looking over the clothes she had brought, she suddenly saw through her own actions. Consciously or not, she had intended to seduce Garrett. The realization of her own unspoken motives sent hot color to her cheeks. Fool, she scolded. What an absolute fool!

At the same time, she felt a sense of freedom.

Tomorrow she would head back home. The next move would have to be Garrett's, not hers. Her trip to Monarch canceled, she could walk with head held high; she was independent and unhindered.

She slipped a white corduroy blazer over the blouse and set off in search of the dining room.

Glory Hole Lodge was built like a wheel, with the rooms forming spokes that radiated from the center, where the lobby, dining room and pool were located. The general style was a comfortable mix of traditional, Western and contemporary.

In the chill of the late-winter dusk, she hurried along the covered lantern-lighted walkway toward the center of the wheel. The cold air cut through her light blazer and she hurried, keeping her head down.

She paused at the dining room entrance. A smiling hostess showed her to a wooden booth at the end of the room. An equally friendly waitress quickly arrived to take her order, and as quickly departed, returning before long with a crockery bowl of French onion soup. Janiver picked up her spoon.

"May I?" he asked, and she looked up and her spoon clattered to the table.

He stood beside her, tall, broad, a faint smile on his lips. His beard was gone, and the difference in his appearance made him seem almost a stranger.

"Garrett!"

He slid onto the bench. He was half turned toward her. Involuntarily she reached out her hand, and he clasped it in both of his.

"I thought it couldn't be you," he said, his eyes devouring her face.

He missed me, her heart sang.

"Your beard—it's gone," she said irrelevantly, touching his cheek with her other hand. He was more handsome without it. "You're different."

"I'd forgotten you've never seen me this way," he said, his eyes still on her face. Had he forgotten how she looked, too?

She hadn't remembered the timbre of his voice, the exact shade of his eyes, the way his hair grew away from his forehead, the breadth of his shoulders.

"What are you doing here?" she asked at last.

"I wanted to get out before the road closed again."

Should she ask why? After all, he hadn't planned to leave before April. Their eyes met, and neither of them looked away.

"Has it been blocked ever since I left?" she managed.

"Every week or so," he told her with a grin. "For the whole seventy-nine days!"

He had counted the days; her heart danced in delight.

"Someone might see," she said, trying to retrieve her hand.

"Who?" he asked. "Art Herbert? Don't worry about Art Herbert. He had a grudge against me, but it's his problem, not mine. The Art Herberts of this world can't really hurt us, no matter what they do. You know that, don't you?"

She nodded, her hand still in his.

"We'll give him a howdy if we should run into him," he said calmly. "Try to look nonchalant." He glanced up to smile politely as the waitress poured a glass of water.

"Don't I?" she asked.

"You look like you just won the state lottery." His voice was gentle as a warm breeze.

So he knew. He could tell by her face how she felt about him. "I had planned to be so calm," she said.

"When?"

"When I saw you," she said.

"Why?" He was enjoying her fluttering embarrassment.

"Why see you, or why be calm?" She was stalling, postponing the very moment she had been waiting for.

"Both."

CHAPTER TEN

THE WAITRESS INTERRUPTED. "Do you intend to order, sir?"

"Please." He accepted a menu and moved to the opposite side of the table. So far away. But he held her hand across the table.

He wasn't wearing his mountain clothes. He was dressed in a navy wool shirt and a navy turtleneck, and he looked fantastic.

His face was more expressive without the beard. The grooves on each side of his mouth deepened as he watched her, his eyes unwavering. When the waitress had collected the menu and taken his order, he held Janiver's hand in both of his, playing with her fingertips.

"Why are you here?" he asked, as though it had just occurred to him that she was out of place.

"The traffic jam," she suggested innocently.

"Where are you going?" he pursued.

"To Denver." He needn't know more.

"Where have you been—Steamboat?" There was an edge to his voice. *Why Steamboat,* she thought. Then she understood.

"Oh, you don't know," she said.

"Know what?"

"Allen and I aren't seeing each other anymore."

Then it was his turn to look the winner. "Oh?" he said carefully.

"It's a long story," she said.

But he didn't care why. "How's the onion soup?" he asked, banishing Allen from their conversation.

"Delicious." But hers had cooled. "Where's Winnie?" she asked.

"With my ranger friend on Shadow Mountain."

Oh, yes, the one he'd stayed with the night they'd said farewell on the pass. She remembered how desperately she had wished he'd come to Monarch with them, how deserted she'd felt.

"Did she miss me?"

"She moped around for weeks," he said.

"Really?"

"No, but I did." She heard the tenderness and the yearning in his voice even though he spoke so softly.

She met his eyes squarely, and saw that he was smiling his knowing smile. She understood—she felt the same way about him. His eyes held her motionless.

"The heck with it," he said, and raised her hand to kiss the palm, slowly, lingeringly.

"Garrett . . ."

"Eat your dinner," he said quietly. "I promise not to bother you."

She shook her head quickly; she didn't want him to stop.

"We have to talk," he said urgently. She knew.

The waitress brought his dinner. Janiver's cold soup was removed and replaced with a large tossed salad.

"Still a model, Janiver?" he asked, smiling with gentle amusement.

"Does it show?"

"Soup and salad?"

"I must keep the tools of my trade in good shape," she quipped. Then she ventured to ask, "Did you get my postcard?"

"The one that didn't say anything?"

"I wrote something," she protested.

"There were some words scribbled on it, but you said nothing."

"What did you expect?" She probed her salad rather too assiduously.

"Something like, 'Having a lousy time . . . wish you were here.'"

"That would have been more to the point, as a matter of fact," she admitted. "Your letter was a masterpiece of nonsense itself."

"I tore up at least ten versions."

"Really?" The picture intrigued her immensely and she smiled with furtive delight.

"Don't laugh," he ordered. "You don't know what I've been through."

"Don't I?" she countered. Had he, then, been through a hell of his own?

"You're heartless." But his face said something different.

They dawdled over dinner, eventually becoming aware of waitresses and busboys hovering impatiently in the background. Except for the two of them, the dining room was empty.

"They want their tips so they can go home," he said.

But she wasn't ready yet to be completely alone with him. All sorts of thoughts flew through her head. Waking in the bed in his cabin; her first sight of him crossing the room toward her; so big, so solid; his calling her 'Laurie,' as though she belonged to him.

She did belong to him. He had saved her life—more than once. He had saved her for himself.

He took her elbow, guided her into the lobby, then hesitated.

"How about a drink?" she stalled.

He gave her a sidelong glance. "Of course." He led the way through the lobby toward the bar, then to a corner table in the darkened room.

Three guitarists standing on a raised platform at the narrower end of the room were playing mellow country blues. With the spotlights focused on the trio, the rest of the lounge was quite dim.

It was not so dim, however, that Art Herbert could not see them—join them immediately after a waitress had taken their order. "Well, what have we here?" His voice was hard as steel.

Garrett stood to shake hands with him, politely gesturing to a chair opposite.

"Garrett Collier and Janiver Parmalee at Glory Hole Lodge—together. Now how does that happen?"

Garrett smiled faintly. "I presume the same traffic jam responsible for our being here also brings you here, Art."

Herbert stared at Janiver. "Perhaps. Then again, perhaps not. The mud slide is not directly responsible for my being here. I knew that if I followed Janiver Parmalee, the trail would lead straight to Garrett Collier."

Garrett's face was stony; his eyes were like flint. "Is there any significance to that remark?"

"You two never fooled me for a minute," Herbert spit out.

"What do you mean?" Janiver exclaimed.

"The dramatic scene on the mountain—it was a hoax, wasn't it? I just can't figure out why. What's the point? Who cares if you two wanted to be together—though I admit my viewers might be interested. But why all the secrecy and all the denials? I've found no jealous husband in Janiver's closet, and Allen Tobin certainly isn't reason enough to carry out that elaborate dramatization. Neither of you needs the publicity. So what's it all for?"

There was silence as the waitress set their drinks on the table.

"When the snow melts, I'll gladly take you to the wreckage myself." Garrett's voice was brittle. "Even better, I suggest you go in with the federal investigators after the spring thaw. It would make a great news story. Might boost your ratings."

Herbert's eyes snapped. "My ratings don't need any help! But if you don't mind, I would like to view the 'crash site.'"

"Fine," Garrett said equably.

Art Herbert stood up and held out his hand, acknowledging that the game was over.

"I wish you luck—both of you," he said grudgingly. "I'll contact the FAA to check into the wreckage." He hadn't completely given in.

Garrett nodded. "Do that," he said.

They watched him scurry through the door to the lobby. "Do you suppose he's rushing out to make a quick phone call to the TV station?" Garrett asked.

"Worms don't use telephones," Janiver said coldly.

Garrett stared at her, then threw back his head and laughed. "You put it very quaintly," he said when he recovered. Clearly he had dismissed Herbert as a minor nuisance.

He bent forward, giving her his full attention. They had some catching up to do—months of it. "After you left the house wasn't the same," he confessed.

She was glad.

"You forgot your nail polish," he pointed out.

"I know."

His hand went to his breast pocket. "You don't have it with you?" she asked incredulously.

"Don't I?"

"Why?"

"How could I know it wasn't the only thing of yours I'd ever have?"

"Garrett." It was a soft wondering protest.

The guitar players were strumming something gentle and slow. He tugged her to her feet. "We've never danced properly," he said, indicating the couples on the dance floor.

She allowed him to pull her close, and it felt completely natural to be held in his arms, to follow his movements. The top of her head fitted comfortably beneath his chin.

"This is as good as the snow cave," he murmured against her hair. She was conscious only of his body and its effect on her own, as she savored his arms around her and surrendered to his lead.

The music stopped and they stood a moment, looking at each other. He still held her, the faintest of smiles on his lips. They were both still under the spell woven by the music and the dance. How had she lived without him all these weeks?

His arm was around her waist as they walked back to their table. "What didn't you say on that ridiculous postcard?" he demanded at last.

She told him about her assignment in the Caribbean—and about meeting Jean DuChamps. At her mention of the Frenchman, Garrett took his hand from hers and studied his beer.

"He said he knew you, Garrett."

"Yes, I know him well. I'll be looking him up this summer when I'm in Paris. Nice fellow. Has a lovely wife, too."

"Paris! Why are you going to Paris?" She didn't care if Jean DuChamps had three lovely wives.

Though she knew Garrett so well in some ways, in others she barely knew him at all. She didn't really know what he did from day to day, for instance, or where he went and why.

He touched her hand again. "It will take years to tell you," he teased, his smile deepening.

His fingers stroked her hand and she drew it quickly away, fearing the flutter aroused in the pit of her stomach.

"Don't go," he said softly.

She raised her eyes to his. "Garrett—"

"Let's get out of here," he said abruptly, throwing some bills on the table and grabbing her arm.

The lobby's bright lights made her blink. There was no one in sight and he halted. "Janiver," he said, and there was a question in the way he spoke her name.

"Hmm?"

"Don't be frightened." As if he understood.

"I could never be afraid, it's just . . ."

"Just . . . ?"

Then she was sorry to be subjecting him to this melodramatic Victorian scene.

"Come to my suite. No strings. We have things to talk over." He was patient and gentle, and of course she would go.

"I'll order coffee," he promised.

She held out her hand and he took it, and they went out a door opposite the one she had come in. They followed a covered walkway similar to the one she had taken earlier that evening—another spoke of the wheel. He guided her up an outside staircase, stopping before a carved wooden door.

"They didn't have anything left except the fancy suites," he said apologetically.

"Too bad for you."

He unlocked the door and stood aside for her to enter. The room was large, far more luxurious than her own.

"How gorgeous!" Janiver exclaimed delightedly, turning around and around to take it all in. "You fared better than I did in your port in a storm." She began to explore the room.

The fireplace wall was paneled with wood laid in a geometric pattern. A long white couch faced the fireplace, and thick rust-colored carpet hugged the floor. Drawn drapes covered one wall. A flight of wooden steps floated upward, presumably to the sleeping loft.

Garrett expertly gathered a handful of kindling and soon had a fire burning brightly, just as he had that last night on Shadow Mountain.

"Will you call room service for coffee?" he asked. She picked up the white telephone and gave instructions.

He rose from kneeling before the hearth. She still stood by the phone, trembling with uncertainty.

"Janiver." He held out both arms.

She came to him instinctively, as though hearing him call her name had somehow released her from indecision.

"I missed you," he said into her hair, his arms crushing her against him.

"Why didn't you write?" she murmured, her eyes closed as she gave herself up to the feel of him.

"I did," he said. Then his lips on hers stopped any further conversation.

She was lost. It was as though she were giving him not only her body but her will.

"Garrett," she whispered, standing on tiptoe, her arms going around his neck, her body pressing against his.

"I love you, Janiver Parmalee." He cradled her in his arms. "I was frantic after you left. Only the snow kept me from getting to Denver before you did."

"I needed time," she confessed. "To know if I'd miss you."

"And did you?" His hand grasped her chin and held it firmly, forcing her to look him straight in the eye.

"Yes," she said faintly.

He drew her down on the couch, kissing her hungrily. She gloried in his strength, his maleness. His caresses urged her body to respond to him. Nothing mattered at that moment except his bidding. Wherever he went, she would follow; whatever he asked, she would do.

"Janiver," he murmured, scooping her into his arms and carrying her toward the stairs.

A discreet knock at the door brought them back to earth. "Damn!" He put her down unceremoniously. She could only stare after him as he opened the door to the room service waiter bearing a tray of coffee.

Garrett took it from him and paid the bill. She giggled at his expression as he carried the tray to the table, grumbling, "Your maidenly honor has been saved for the moment—by room service, of all things."

Janiver sat close beside him on the couch and reached for a cup. "One never knows when one's knight in shining armor will appear, or in what guise," she said lightly.

"Don't forget the Oriental tradition. You're responsible for my happiness for the rest of my life," he reminded her, speaking quite seriously.

"I'll work on it," she said, her lips trembling.

He turned her to face him. "Every happiness," he said, his mouth curving up at the corners. "Forever."

"Garrett," she whispered, wanting him to continue.

But he let her go. He picked up his cup, then asked abruptly "Did DuChamps offer you a job?"

She was nerve ends and emotions, nothing else. She was so aware of him beside her that she couldn't think straight. "Yes," she said. "Yes, he did."

She expected one further question: Had she accepted? But he did not ask.

"It's the opportunity of a lifetime," he lectured. "And I'll be in Paris in a few weeks. Give me your address there...."

She looked at him warily. He was staring into the fire, where little blue flames licked steadily at the remains of a log.

"Garrett," she began.

The telephone rang, cutting off the words that might have set everything right.

She handed him the phone. "It would never do for a woman to answer," she said softly.

He grinned, lightly touching the tip of her nose with his forefinger. "Yes?" he spoke into the receiver, but his eyes never left her face.

She half listened to his side of the conversation; it sounded strictly business.

When she started to get up to wander to the window, he grasped her wrist firmly, pulling her close to his side.

"I haven't heard," he was saying. There was a pause. Then he said, "Make the decision, Mark. I'll stand behind you. Let me know what happens, and call me in the morning."

She turned toward him then, and he slid his hands to the small of her back, fitting her body to his. "Garrett," she began, but he wasn't listening. His face was warm against her neck, and she could feel his lips moving just beneath her ear.

"You can have one year at DuChamps," he said authoritatively. "Then you're mine." Her pulse raced; her heart thundered in her ears.

"Don't you want me now?" she asked faintly against his cheek.

He hugged her so tightly against him that she couldn't breathe. "Want you? I've wanted you ever since poor battered Sleeping Beauty lay in my bed. Remember, I didn't want you to leave."

"Then shut up and listen for a minute!" she commanded, putting her hand over his mouth. "You talk too much, Garrett Collier! I have not accepted a job with Jean—nor do I intend to. I was coming to see you. If you expect to see me in Paris, you'll be disappointed. My address will be Colorado—all summer."

Slowly she took her hand away from his mouth. He stared at her, unbelieving. "What do you say to that?" She smiled gently as she looked into his eyes.

"You're not going?" He was dumbfounded. "You were coming to see *me*?"

She nodded vigorously, her eyes dancing.

"Why?" he asked, and his face went still.

"Because I love you, you dope!"

"Are you sure?" he asked quietly.

"Absolutely!" She threw her arms around him and melted against him. He met her halfway and they fell back on the cushions.

"Damn room service," he muttered after a time.

"You're too easily discouraged," she whispered, tracing the outline of his mouth with her fingertips.

He brushed his lips against her lips lightly, then drew firmly away from her. "No, Janiver, we'll do this right. No regrets. After a while I'll walk you to your room—and come back alone."

Tears threatened to spill from her eyes. He didn't want her! Misery such as she had never known squeezed an icy fist around her heart.

"Garrett!" she pleaded.

"Where will the wedding be?" he asked. "And when?"

Wedding? She hadn't expected that. She knew only that she wanted to be with him now and as far into the future as she could imagine. Without Garrett she had no future, and no present, either.

She sat up straight, her hair tangled around her face. "I hadn't been thinking about about marriage," she said slowly.

"Well, now you are," he said. "I didn't say anything before because I didn't want to rush you. I had to know how you felt. My own feelings I was sure of. I've never believed in love at first sight, but it didn't take any longer than that for me to fall in love with you. Even though you slept through our first two days together, I...I was obsessed by you. I couldn't help it. I wanted to know how you talked, how you laughed, what you liked and disliked—everything about you."

"And were you disappointed?" she asked.

"No."

So while they finished the coffee and cookies, they discussed marriage—their marriage. With wonder, and with the joy of discovering each other. It was not yet real, but something that had to be talked about over and over before she could begin to believe it.

She snuggled against him. "Weddings are scary, Garrett. All those people!"

"Witnesses to your commitment," he said sternly.

"It would be simpler if I just moved into your apartment."

"No." He shook his head. "We won't start that way. We'll start our life together in the best way possible."

"You're very sweet." She smiled, lightly touching his lips.

"Don't tempt me!" he warned.

A short time later they walked back to her room. He cupped her face in his hands and kissed her softly. "I'll see you for breakfast," he said.

"Good night, my love." She didn't want him to leave. Laughing, he took her by the shoulders and propelled her through the door, then walked resolutely away.

Dazed, she undressed slowly for bed. She lay awake a long time, her thoughts marching around and around in her head, until at last, exhausted, she slept.

She was awakened by the jangling of the telephone. She rested the receiver on the pillow beside her. "Hello?"

"Good morning, my darling."

"Garrett!" She smiled and stretched luxuriously, like a satisfied kitten.

"I couldn't sleep," he said. "I'll be there in five minutes with coffee."

"From room service?" she asked.

"Hey! I see you're alert even at this early hour."

"You should remember how alert I am."

"I remember everything about you!"

"You think!" she dared, then blushed, remembering how intimate their relationship had been before she had ever even seen him.

"Test me when I get there!" He hung up.

She sat straight up in the middle of the bed, all of the previous night jumbling about her. A minute or so later he came in, brisk and energetic and full of plans. He leaned over to kiss her thoroughly before even setting down the coffeepot.

"Wake up, sleepyhead! We've got things to do, places to go!"

"We can't go together—we've got two cars. My father will be furious if I don't return his little treasure in mint condition."

He sat down on the bed, his eyes resting a moment on her lace-covered breasts, then moving slowly back to her face. He reached out to tousle her hair, smiling mysteriously. For an instant she was reminded of the way he'd looked that one night in the cabin. But his wistful expression changed to one of supreme satisfaction.

"Believe it or not, I ran into a friend who needs a ride. He'll drive my car and we'll take yours."

That settled that.

She relaxed against the plumped pillows, cradling her coffee cup in both hands. "Now about this wedding," she began.

"Our wedding," he corrected, moving closer to kiss her bare shoulder.

A MONTH LATER Janiver stood poised at the rear of the church as the organ began the strains of the processional. Light from the stained glass windows filtered across the crowded pews.

Her dress was a designer's masterpiece, simply cut, the fabric elegant. It molded her figure beautifully. A demiveil anchored by a circlet of pearls and tulle fell in a misty cloud to her shoulders. Her pale hair was arranged in a classic chignon, emphasizing the graceful neck curving into the line of her high breasts.

Garrett and his groomsmen waited at the altar in pearl-gray morning suits. As each bridesmaid reached him, Garrett smiled politely. Then his eyes would return impatiently to where Janiver stood, her hand tucked into the curve of her father's arm.

Garrett and her father had liked each other immediately, just as she'd expected they would.

The music quickened and her father squeezed her hand. When Janiver turned to kiss him on the cheek, there were tears in his eyes.

"I love him," she whispered. He nodded, and then they started the long walk that would end with her as Garrett's wife.

She liked the idea of belonging to Garrett, of having Garrett belong to her.

Then she was standing beside him and he was looking down at her in relief—as if he'd thought she'd never get there. He firmly took her hand from her father's arm and tucked it around his.

The minister's words were solemn, traditional. She repeated the same vows said by countless brides, watched as Garrett slipped the wide gold band onto her finger. When the ceremony was finished they walked down the aisle together.

Outside, Channel 15 cameramen mingled with a knot of onlookers. Garrett's hand tightened on hers.

"Smile!" he murmured in her ear. "You're a star!" He strode directly up to Art Herbert and held out his hand. Herbert looked pleased, signaled for the cameras to keep turning and shook Garrett's extended hand. At last he had the ending to the story that had begun on Shadow Mountain.

Then Garrett was opening the door of the silver Rolls Royce that would carry them to the reception.

"Garrett, you're wonderful!" she exclaimed.

Beside her, he said with a grin, "And don't you forget it, Laurie Collier!"

IT WAS DUSK when they finally left the reception. She had changed into a lavender suit with a matching blouse in a darker shade. Garrett held the door of his sports car open for her, then came around and got behind the wheel.

"Well, hello, Mrs. Collier," he said softly, turning to kiss her.

"You look like the cat that swallowed the canary," she remarked.

He raised his eyebrows mischievously. "I'm about to." He switched on the ignition and swung the low sleek automobile into the stream of westbound traffic.

"This trauma hasn't been too much for you?"

"I think I'm going to like it," she admitted.

"If I didn't have such a compulsive nature, we'd turn around this minute and go straight to my apartment," he said.

"I told you that would be simpler than getting married," she said, smiling.

"You sound like you've done that before," he said. "Have you?" he pursued.

She shook her head. "Never, but I was willing to with you."

"My point was that no matter what you might have done in the past, I wanted you to be my wife."

She put her hand on his arm. "You are a complete romantic."

"Is that bad?"

"It's marvelous."

"My real reason for insisting on marriage was so you couldn't get away."

"Oh, now I see it all! That's the reason you wanted me locked in."

"Exactly!"

"Silly!" She reached up to touch his cheek, but he caught her hand and kissed the palm.

"Kick off your shoes and make yourself comfortable," he suggested.

"How long will this safari take?" she asked.

"No more than two hours."

She lay back, relaxing, as the car ran deeper and deeper into the dark mountains. Garrett reached for her hand, stroked her fingers. They talked comfortably of the wedding, of guests, of anything and everything.

"Did anyone ever tell you you're very special?" she asked him.

"I don't believe anyone ever has. Do you know someone who feels that way?"

"Most definitely," she murmured, caressing his hand with her thumb.

"Janiver Parmalee Collier, take it easy!" he protested.

She smiled confidently, then closed her eyes, shifted slightly toward him in the seat.

The next thing she knew, he was gently shaking her awake. "Janiver!"

She saw at once where they were. "Garrett! This is Glory Hole Lodge!"

"Imagine!" He answered with a grin.

The lights in the lobby cast a golden welcome, hinting at the comfortable charm of the place. It had never occurred to her that he might bring her back here.

He held her close as they registered, then climbed the outside staircase to the suite, where he fumbled with the lock on the heavy wooden door with his free hand.

A low fire burned in the fireplace, shedding a cozy glow on the room. Garrett shut the door and turned the bolt. He had planned ahead; a tray with coffee and cookies waited on the low table.

She ran to him and, almost shyly, put her arms around his neck. "Garrett, I love you so," she whispered.

"No regrets?" he asked.

She shook her head, a smile of delight on her face. "None," she said solemnly, standing on tiptoes to kiss his lips.

He picked her up in his arms and started toward the stairs. "Now to finish some interrupted business," he said tenderly, purposefully.

"And high time, too," she murmured against his neck.

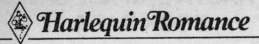 **Harlequin Romance**

Coming Next Month

2791 HUNTER'S SNARE Emily Ruth Edwards
Faking an engagement to protect her boss from an old flame
seems an outrageous idea for a secretary—until she needs
protection of her own from Connecticut's most dynamic
new businessman.

2792 IMPRESSIONS Tracy Hughes
A Manhattan image consultant has trouble finding the right
look for the host of the TV network's new public affairs show.
Her client thinks he's just fine the way he is—for the network
and for her!

2793 SEPARATE LIVES Carolyn Jantz
Their financial problems were solved by marriage, and love
was an added bonus. Now doubts and the very contract that
brought them together threaten to drive them apart.

2794 CALL OF THE MOUNTAIN Miriam MacGregor
The faster an editor completes her assignment, the faster she
can leave behind a New Zealand station and her boss's
ridiculous accusations. If only his opinion of her wasn't
so important....

2795 IMPULSIVE CHALLENGE Margaret Mayo
When a secretary, who has no illusions about her "love 'em and
leave 'em" boss, finds herself jealous of his glamorous
neighbor, she's shocked. She's fallen in love—the thing she
vowed never to do again.

2796 SAFARI HEARTBREAK Gwen Westwood
This mother doesn't object to her son's yearly visits to his
father, until her mother-in-law's illness forces her into making
the trek back to Africa—scene of her greatest heartbreak...her
greatest happiness.

Available in October wherever paperback books are sold, or
through Harlequin Reader Service.

In the U.S.
P.O. Box 1397
Buffalo, N.Y.
14240-1397

In Canada
P.O. Box 2800, Postal Station A
5170 Yonge Street
Willowdale, Ontario M2N 6J3

Where passion and destiny meet . . .
there is love

Jesse's Lady

Veronica Sattler

Brianna Deveraux had a feisty spirit matched by that of only one man, Jesse Randall. In North Carolina, 1792, they dared to forge a love as vibrant and alive as life in their bold new land.